Une faim d'éléphant

Texte de Kate Walker

Illustrations d'Ann James

Texte français de Brigitte Surreau

Éditions
SCHOLASTIC

Copyright © Kate Walker, 1998, pour le texte.

Copyright © Ann James, 1998, pour les illustrations.

Conception graphique de la couverture :
Lyn Mitchell.

Copyright © Éditions Scholastic, 2006,
pour le texte français. Tous droits réservés.

Texte original publié par Omnibus Books,
de SCHOLASTIC GROUP, Sydney, Australie.

Catalogage avant publication de Bibliothèque
et Archives Canada

Walker, Kate
Une faim d'éléphant / Kate Walker;
illustrations d'Ann James;
texte français de Brigitte Surreau.
(Petit roman)

Traduction de : Elephant's Lunch.
Niveau d'intérêt selon l'âge :
Pour enfants de 7 à 9 ans.
ISBN 0-439-94079-6

I. James, Ann II. Surreau, Brigitte, 1958- III. Titre.

PZ23.W35Fai 2006   823'.914   C2005-906707-1

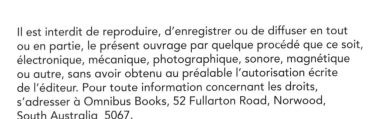

Édition publiée par les Éditions Scholastic, 175 Hillmount Road,
Markham (Ontario) L6C 1Z7 CANADA.

6 5 4 3 2 1   Imprimé au Canada   06 07 08 09

À ma grand-mère – K.W.

À Leonie Gaff et toute la bande – A.J.

Chapitre 1

Clara regarde dans son sac
d'école et fronce les sourcils.

— Es-tu sûre de m'avoir mis
assez à manger pour dîner?
demande-t-elle à sa mère.

— Assez à manger! s'exclame sa mère. Quatre sandwichs au beurre d'arachide, six bananes, un morceau de gâteau au chocolat et de la tarte aux pommes!

— Mais je dois rester à l'école toute la journée et je vais avoir horriblement faim! s'exclame Clara.

— Tu n'auras pas faim, affirme sa mère, c'est impossible. Tu as assez dans ton sac pour rassasier un éléphant! Maintenant, allons-y.

Chapitre 2

Clara et sa mère marchent
jusqu'au quai pour attendre
le traversier.

Pendant que sa mère discute avec d'autres personnes, Clara va parler à l'éléphant qu'elle a vu attendre aussi.

Il est gros et gris, avec de petits yeux très doux.

— Bonjour! dit Clara.

L'éléphant cligne des yeux, puis regarde l'eau, au loin.

Clara regarde aussi. Elle voit
des remorqueurs, des pétroliers et
des yachts. Mais pas de traversier.

— Attends-tu le traversier?
demande-t-elle.

L'éléphant ne répond pas.

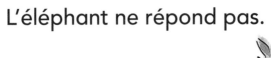

— Un jour, j'attendais le traversier, dit Clara, et il était en retard. J'avais horriblement faim. Tellement faim que mon ventre grondait et me faisait très mal. J'espère que tu n'as pas faim; tu as un super gros ventre et tu aurais super mal.

De nouveau, l'éléphant ne répond rien. Mais Clara voit qu'il a les oreilles basses.

Chapitre 3

Clara sait très bien ce que c'est qu'attendre le traversier et comme ça donne faim. Plus faim qu'attendre l'autobus ou encore que le feu passe au vert.

Pauvre éléphant!

Il devrait avoir quelque chose
à manger, juste au cas où le
traversier serait en retard.

Clara ouvre son sac d'école. Les éléphants aiment les arachides, tout le monde le sait.

Elle prend un sandwich au
beurre d'arachide et le lui tend.

L'éléphant cligne seulement des
yeux.

— Mmmmm! du beurre
d'arachide! dit Clara en se
frottant le ventre.

L'éléphant cligne encore des
yeux. Il ne comprend pas.

MIAM!
MIAM! MIAM!

Chapitre 4

Pour expliquer à l'éléphant ce qu'elle veut dire, Clara mange le premier sandwich en mastiquant avec beaucoup de bruit.

Ensuite, elle sort le deuxième sandwich. Mais, comme avant, l'éléphant cligne des yeux et ne dit pas un mot.

Ce sont peut-être les singes qui aiment les arachides, pense Clara. Puis elle mange le deuxième sandwich avec de grands « Mmm! Mmm! », en roulant les yeux.

Mais l'éléphant ne semble toujours pas comprendre.

Clara mange le troisième
sandwich et passe sa langue sur
ses lèvres.

— Mmmmmm! fait-elle.

L'éléphant lève la trompe et
se gratte l'oreille.

Il n'est peut-être pas très malin, pense Clara.

Elle sort le quatrième sandwich et déclare :

— Si tu ne manges pas ce délicieux sandwich au beurre d'arachide, moi, je vais le manger!

L'éléphant ne répond rien; il laisse juste pendre sa trompe.

— C'est ta dernière chance, dit
Clara en portant le sandwich à sa
bouche.

— C'est ta deuxième dernière
chance, dit Clara en ouvrant tout
grand la bouche.

— C'est ta troisième dernière chance, dit Clara, qui mord enfin dans le sandwich.

L'éléphant regarde au loin.
Le dernier sandwich au beurre
d'arachide a été avalé.

Chapitre 5

Clara regarde l'eau. Il y a des
hors-bord, des chaloupes et
un catamaran. Mais pas de
traversier.

— Tu ne sais peut-être pas ça, fait remarquer Clara à l'éléphant, mais certains traversiers sont tellement en retard qu'ils ne viennent même pas. Tu auras horriblement mal au ventre alors.

L'éléphant laisse retomber ses épaules..

Il commence à comprendre, maintenant, pense Clara.

Elle ouvre son sac et en sort six bananes.

C'est un très gros éléphant.
Il pourrait les manger toutes.
Alors elle les pèle et les dispose
sur le banc à côté de lui.

Mais l'éléphant reste là à
regarder l'eau.

Peut-être que ce sont les gorilles qui aiment les bananes, pense Clara.

Maintenant que les bananes sont pelées, quelqu'un doit les manger. Alors Clara les mange.

— Tu es l'animal le plus difficile que j'ai jamais rencontré, dit-elle à l'éléphant. Si le traversier n'arrive pas, tu auras super mal au ventre tellement tu auras faim.

Chapitre 6

Clara regarde dans son sac
d'école encore une fois.
— Tu aimes sûrement le gâteau
au chocolat, dit-elle.

Le monde entier aime le gâteau au chocolat! Les mamans et les papas, les souris et les perroquets, les chats et les chiens.

Clara regarde l'eau. Elle voit un bateau à aubes et quelques kayaks. Mais pas de traversier.

— Bon, déclare-t-elle. Je vais partager mon gâteau au chocolat avec toi.

Elle partage le gâteau en deux et en pose un morceau sur le banc, à côté de l'éléphant.

Elle s'apprête à remettre l'autre morceau dans son sac, mais avant, il faut qu'elle en prenne une petite bouchée.

Puis une autre.

Puis encore une autre.

Maintenant, il ne reste plus qu'une bouchée. Inutile d'ouvrir son sac pour si peu!

Clara met le dernier morceau dans sa bouche.

C'est alors qu'elle entend
Touuut! Touuut!

C'est le traversier! L'éléphant
ne sera pas affamé, après tout.

Chapitre 7

Vite, Clara saisit le morceau de
gâteau destiné à l'éléphant, en
pensant à tous les gens du monde
qui aiment le chocolat, eux aussi.
Les mamies et les papis, les
grandes sœurs, les petits frères,
les professeurs, les policiers, tout
le monde!

Touuut! Le traversier s'arrête
au bord du quai, et Clara voit que
l'éléphant a disparu. Le morceau
de gâteau au chocolat qu'elle
avait dans la main aussi.

Maintenant, tout ce qu'il lui reste pour son repas, c'est une toute petite tarte aux pommes.

Oh! là! là! je vais avoir horriblement faim, se dit Clara. Comme la fois où j'ai attendu le traversier et qu'il n'est pas venu. Mon ventre va gronder et me faire mal.

Chapitre 8

Clara se ressaisit vite.

Elle engloutit la tarte aux pommes pour que son sac d'école soit léger, puis elle dit à sa mère :

— Vite, nous devons rentrer à la maison et prendre plus à manger.

Elle montre son sac vide.

Sa mère n'en croit pas ses yeux.

— Clara! s'écrie-t-elle, où est le dîner que je t'ai préparé?

— Je l'ai mangé, répond Clara, il le fallait. Il y avait cet éléphant gris, tu sais… qui attendait le traversier, et…

— Ah! aujourd'hui, c'était un éléphant, dit sa mère.

— Oui, un gros, réplique Clara.

— Ce n'était pas un gorille?
demande sa mère.

— Non, dit Clara. Le gorille,
c'était hier.

— Et pas un singe, non plus?
interroge sa mère.

— Tu ne te souviens pas?
répond Clara. J'ai rencontré le
singe le jour d'avant.

Sa mère secoue la tête.

— Clara, je ne sais pas où tu mets toute cette nourriture.

— Dans mon ventre, bien sûr! s'exclame Clara. Ainsi, il ne grondera pas et ne me fera pas mal.

— Eh bien, je n'aime pas dire ce genre de choses, Clara, fait remarquer sa mère, mais tu manges comme un éléphant.

— Ce n'est pas vrai! s'écrie Clara. Je me suis rendu compte que les éléphants ne mangent vraiment pas beaucoup.

Et les chameaux non plus d'ailleurs, comme Clara s'en rend compte sur le chemin de l'école, le lendemain!

Kate Walker

Les éléphants sont mes animaux préférés. Peut-être parce que le tout premier petit roman que j'ai lu parlait d'un garçon qui était devenu l'ami d'un éléphant de la jungle. Tous deux s'entraidaient. Ils étaient les meilleurs amis du monde. Après cela, j'ai lu tous les livres que j'ai pu trouver à la bibliothèque sur les éléphants.

Ou peut-être que j'aime les éléphants parce qu'ils me rappellent ma grand-mère. C'était une dame corpulente, très ridée, avec des petits yeux pleins de douceur. Elle se balançait d'un côté à l'autre en marchant. Je ne lui ai jamais dit qu'elle me faisait penser à un éléphant, car j'aurais pu la blesser, mais c'était vraiment le cas!

Ann James

Je me suis beaucoup amusée quand j'ai dessiné les illustrations de ce livre. Je trouve que l'idée de discuter avec un éléphant en attendant le traversier est tout à fait charmante.

Quand j'attends le traversier, le tramway ou le train, j'aime observer tout ce qu'il y a autour de moi, surtout les gens et les animaux. Parfois, j'invente des histoires sur eux, dans ma tête – où ils vivent, pourquoi ils ont l'air heureux ou triste.

J'ai souvent faim, aussi, quand j'attends, mais personne n'a jamais partagé son repas avec moi – du moins, pas encore!

BOOK 1 OF

THE YELLOW HOODS

ALONG CAME A WOLF

AN EMERGENT STEAMPUNK SERIES
BY ADAM DREECE

ADZO Publishing Inc.

Calgary, Canada

ADZO Publishing Inc.
Calgary, Alberta, Canada
www.adzopublishing.com

Edited by: Chris W. Rea, Jennifer Zouak
Printed in Canada

Library and Archives Canada Cataloguing in Publication

Dreece, Adam, 1972-, author
        Along came a wolf / written by Adam Dreece.

(The Yellow hoods ; bk. 1)
Issued in print and electronic formats.
ISBN 978-0-9881013-0-2 (pbk.).--ISBN 978-0-9881013-1-9 (epub)

I. Title. II. Series: Dreece, Adam, 1972-. Yellow Hoods ; bk.1.
PS8607.R39A84 2014   jC813'.6   C2014-901592-5
                                  C2014-901593-3

4   5   6   7   8   9 3/9/16 35,261

Library of Congress information available upon request.

DEDICATION

To my daughter, for her enthusiasm
for the story, and
encouragement to write it,

To my sons, for keeping the
little boy in me thriving,

and

To my wife, without whose
anchoring force
I'd be lost in the wind.

CHAPTERS

EORTHE

Cartographer: Driss of Zouak, 1793
Created at the behest of the Council of Southern
Kingdoms

CHAPTER ONE
COMING
THROUGH

"Watch out!" yelled Tee.

Her gleeful voice could barely be heard over the sounds of her wooden contraption crashing down the forested mountainside.

A short distance away, Tee's mother, Jennifer, looked up from her tomato garden. She wiped her forehead and looked at her husband, William. "What has your daughter gone and done now?" she said. Their daughter certainly kept life exciting.

"She's *your* daughter, too," said William. He was a tall, thin man with light brown hair, and a beard. He quickly tossed aside his axe and started hunting around the side of their cabin for the tool he'd need.

"Oh, William, love, I think she's more yours in habits, if you ask me."

"Watch out!" Tee gleefully yelled again. She was rapidly approaching the clearing surrounding their log cabin home.

Jennifer stood and looked in the direction of Tee's voice. She couldn't imagine how Tee was coming down the mountainside so fast. "Will—I'm worried she's coming faster than usual."

"Faster than the time with the pony? Now where did I leave my—"

"Somehow, yes. I'm wondering if she's built something this time." Jennifer furrowed her brow.

"Humph—I can't find it! Where *is* it?"

Jennifer paused. "Oh! It's hanging inside the front door. I put it there this morning. Sorry!"

William darted to the door and grabbed his crossbow. "There we go! Do you have the bolt with the rope attached?"

Jennifer tried to track where Tee was, using the swaying bushes and trees as indicators. "It should be in the quiver—the case thing... whatever you call it. Check by the spare saddles."

"Right! I was going to put them in the shed this morning. Why didn't I put them in the shed?" William raced across the yard and grabbed the bolt he needed.

Jennifer nervously moved from side to side. "Hurry up! I think you've got less than half a minute before she's here."

William fought to untangle the rope, glancing up every few seconds.

Suddenly, Tee popped into view. "*Wheee!* Hi Mom!" she said. Tee was clutching the steering wheel of her cart; a ripped bed sheet hung from its broken mast. Her yellow cloak flapped in the wind behind her.

"Got it!" said William. He loaded his crossbow and aimed at Tee's cart as she rocketed past.

"Shoot already, Will!" said Jennifer, realizing their daughter might end up sailing right off the nearby cliff.

William took a deep breath. Just as his daughter reached the end of the clearing, he pulled the trigger. After a moment, there came a wood-splintering crash, and then silence.

Jennifer looked at her husband in horror. "Oh my —"

William waved for her to stay calm. "Tee!" he called loudly. "Can you get yourself down?" he asked, trying to sound confident. Worry started to creep across his face.

After an agonizing few seconds, there came some rustling sounds and Tee replied, "I think so, Dad. Give me a moment... Yeah! I'm okay."

Then, with practiced flare, Tee jumped into the clearing and yelled her trademark, "La-la!"

Jennifer turned and looked at William with a mix of relief and frustration. "How many more years until I don't have to worry about her?"

"Forever and a day, my love," said William, smiling. "Forever and a day."

———————

Tee woke up to the familiar sound of the kettle whistling and the table being set. She sat up and yawned, unaware of the adventure that lay ahead.

Her first attempt to join the family for breakfast was rebuffed. As usual, her mother informed her that she needed to brush her shoulder-length dark brown hair before sitting at the table. After huffing about it for a minute, Tee went to brush her hair.

To her mother's surprise, Tee had even dressed herself before returning. Looking ready for the day, Tee complained, "Why do you *always* make me brush my hair before breakfast?"

Her mother got the scrambled eggs out of the cast-iron skillet, sat herself down, and turned to her daughter. "You *know* why. But, you won't need to brush your hair anymore if—"

"Really?" Tee interrupted.

Pushing back her own dark curly hair, Jennifer continued, "*if* you find a magical way to make it unknot itself."

"Mo-omm! There's no such thing as magic." Tee plunked herself into a chair and looked at her dad, expecting him to say something.

Jennifer turned to her husband and smirked. "Am I being unreasonable, Will?"

William looked at his wife, and then his daughter, each awaiting his involvement. Having learned his lesson from this type of situation before, he quickly put a piece of toast in his mouth and looked elsewhere. The conversation eventually moved on without his input.

With the dishes collected and all signs of breakfast gone, Tee leapt for her yellow hooded cloak and backpack, both hanging by the door, when her dad stepped in the way.

"Tee, before you vanish for the day, I need you to do something for me. I have something that needs to be delivered to Grandpapa. If you could help your mother while I ..." William deliberately paused, anticipating Tee's interruption.

Tee jumped at the opportunity. Unleashing her huge brown eyes—her best weapons of influence—she asked, "Can I take it to him?"

She loved visiting her mom's father. Apart from being kind and patient, he was a marvelous inventor and loved explaining things to her. He also made the best cookies, and always seemed to have some ready as she walked in. When asked how he knew she was coming, he'd always smile and change the subject.

William pretended to think over his daughter's proposal. "Well... I *was* going to take it to his house while you helped your mother weed the garden and clean the house, but if you insist—"

"I insist!" she yelled so loudly that she startled herself. She looked around for a package to deliver.

William smiled. He loved his daughter dearly. For all the trouble she got into, there was never anything but good intentions.

"Actually, it's in the shed. There's a set of plant pots. One is turned upside down—"

"I know the one! It was turned over yesterday morning. I thought that was odd." Tee raced off.

"It's a little red box!" yelled William, shaking his head. He was surprised she knew what he was talking about. It seemed impossible to hide anything from her.

He snapped his fingers, having almost forgotten he was Tee's father. "Remember," he shouted, "to stay on the roads—and don't talk to strangers!"

"I will," shouted a little voice from the distance.

William looked at his wife as she came in carrying an armload of firewood. "I just passed a little yellow whirlwind. What was that about?" she asked.

"The package that arrived yesterday for your father—Tee's going to deliver it."

"Couldn't he have picked it up this evening when he comes for dinner?" asked Jennifer.

William looked out the front window. "No. I figure if there's any trouble to come of it, it'll come to us today. Best that she's not here," he answered.

Jennifer frowned for a moment. "Do you think that's safe?"

William turned as if he saw something in the forest. "I just—I have a bad feeling. Hopefully this will keep her out of trouble."

Jennifer's eyes took on a steely glint. She straightened up, her posture revealing a hint of the hidden warrior within. "Do you know what's in that red box?"

"No," he replied, "but I have a good idea."

CHAPTER TWO
OF WOLVES &
PIGS

Tee placed the little red box in her backpack, slipped the backpack over her shoulders, and then pulled her cloak over top. With her parcel secured, she proceeded to sing and dance down the road, as she usually did.

She loved the smell of the forest, and the look of the red and yellow leaves everywhere. It was like a duel of colors, each fighting for supremacy.

While autumn had just begun, the trees seemed a bit impatient to embrace winter. Every now and then, the morning seemed to whisper that winter wasn't far away. Tee wondered what the rush was.

"Hello. Well, what do we have here?" boomed a menacing, local-accented voice. Instinctively, Tee sprang into the bushes. After a quick look around, she realized the voice came from down the road.

The voice belonged to a tall, rough-looking, unshaven man. He was about fifty yards down the trail with two bigger, rougher-looking men, one on each side. The trio had stopped a finely dressed man atop a brown and white horse.

Tee moved through the bushes with practiced ease, until she could clearly see the three men. "The Cochon brothers," she muttered to herself. She'd heard of the troublemakers and had been warned many times to avoid them. There were rumors they'd recently run some guys out of town.

The stranger's horse nervously moved back and forth, trying to get away from the brothers who flanked her. The rider was doing his best to keep her calm.

"Let me pass," said the rider in crisp, clear words.

Tee immediately noticed his slight accent, and the way he held himself. By the way he was looking down at the ruffians, and how his words were clear and sharply pronounced, she guessed he was used to being around important people—perhaps even royalty. Her grandfather had taught her how to listen for such clues.

She wondered if the rider was from one of the two capital cities of their small kingdom, or maybe even from one of the neighboring kingdoms to the east or south.

"I have an urgent message to deliver. Remove yourselves!" he commanded, placing his hand atop the gold and silver hilt of his sword. A flintlock pistol was visible, tucked into his black belt.

Tee shook her head. "Shouldn't have said that," she muttered to herself. "Now they're going to want what you've got."

The two younger brothers looked to the eldest, who stood in front of the horse. "I'll tell you what, *messenger boy*," said the eldest Cochon. "For a small sum of money, I'll deliver the message for you. Now what is it?"

The rider closely examined the three brothers. "My name is Andre LeLoup. I am on official business. Out of my way!" he said indignantly. He seemed both relieved and disappointed that they didn't recognize his name.

"That's a funny name for a horse—*official business!*" said the middle brother, known as Squeals. The three brothers laughed.

"Right you are," said the eldest. "Right you are. Now, I'm not an unreasonable man. Am I, Bore?"

The youngest brother, Bore, was by far the largest.

A wall of a man, he stood six feet, five inches tall. Like his brothers, his clothes were homemade, and badly. Worse yet, his boots were a patchwork, made by cutting up pairs of smaller boots and stitching them together.

He shook his head in an exaggerated fashion and replied in a deep, dim-witted voice, "No, Bakon, nope."

Bore's first name was actually Boris, but he had never been able to pronounce it properly. Everyone knew him as Bore. Unfortunately, it emphasized his pig-like looks. "My brother, he's a nice man," he added, giggling like a mischievous little boy.

Meanwhile, in the bushes, Tee rifled through her backpack.

Bakon studied the messenger up and down. "So, how about you come down for a little chat then, eh?" he asked.

The messenger glared at the ruffians and started to reach for his pistol. "Now, I demand—"

Bakon interrupted, "Oh, I've had enough of him. Bring him down, boys!"

On command, the two Cochon brothers reached up and pulled the man down with ease, forcing him to his knees and holding him in place.

Squeals slapped the horse's side, yelling, "Get out of here!"

Bakon looked at Squeals in disbelief as the horse ran away. "What did you do that for? We could have sold it! Or maybe the message was on it!"

Squeals' head slumped in submission. "Oh—sorry, Bakon. Wasn't thinking."

Bore also shook his head. "No thinking, Squeals. No thinking," he said, tapping the side of his head. Squeals gave Bore a look that put him in his place.

Bakon quickly calmed himself down. "She won't go far. Just... *don't* do that next time." He then turned to the messenger. "So, Monsieur ..." he started, trying to remember the messenger's name.

The messenger glared up from his forced kneeling position, his arms pinned by the two huge brothers. "My name is LeLoup. This is an insult! I will have you —"

Bakon waved at the man to stop talking. "What is it you want out of this? Do you want to hand over the message? Or maybe you'd like to hand over your gold *and* the message? I couldn't blame you if you wanted to do that, now, could I?"

The two brothers nodded in agreement.

"I'd like for you to drop dead!" spat LeLoup.

Suddenly, Bakon fell over—flat on his face.

Bore and Squeals looked at each other in a panic and screamed, "Aaah! Magic!" They ran off into the forest.

Tee reloaded her slingshot and jumped out of the bushes. "La-la!" she yelled triumphantly. "Run away, little piggies!" She quickly scanned the forest for more trouble.

Once she confirmed no one else was lurking, she lowered her slingshot and approached the messenger. He was angrily talking to himself.

Tee pointed to the face-down elder Cochon brother and said, "He'll be up in a minute. The stones I use only stun for a couple of minutes at most."

The messenger finished brushing himself off. He scrutinized Tee, in her yellow hooded cloak, white blouse, and light brown pants. He wrinkled his nose at how boyishly she dressed.

"So, you are the one who knocked out the ruffian?" he asked.

"Tee, Yellow Hood of the forest, at your service," she replied, bowing. Andre shook his head slightly at her lack of a curtsey.

"I am Andre LeLoup. A pleasure to meet you," he said stiffly. "Thank you for your assistance. I thought

I'd seen a flash of yellow in the distance. I didn't realize it was a person. Never mind—you are my little savior, are you not?" He offered an appreciative smile. "But, if you don't mind, I'd prefer to keep this between us. It won't help my reputation for people to learn that I was helped by a little girl in a yellow hood."

Tee smiled. "You know your name means *wolf*, right?"

"Of course I know that," he replied firmly. He found his hat and dusted it off.

Tee leaned in. "And… you were just assaulted by the *Cochon* brothers," she said, nodding knowingly.

Andre looked about to see if any of his other belongings had fallen to the ground during the commotion. "Oh—was that their name?"

Tee giggled.

"What is it?" asked Andre, turning to her, annoyed.

Tee pulled her hood over her face. "Nothing—it's just, you know… never mind." She finished her giggling and took a deep breath. "Okay—sorry. So, where are you trying to go?"

Andre put his hat on and then straightened his mustache. "I am sorry. I appreciate your assistance, but it's official business and I can't say. Now, do you think I have any chance of finding my horse, or should I continue into town on foot?"

Tee looked around to get her bearings. "I'm sure we can find her. She probably went over to the nearby clearing. This road leads there. It's only about five minutes if we take the shortcut."

Bakon started to make noises and moved a hand to rub the back of his head.

"We should go—now," Tee whispered. She grabbed Andre by the hand and led him into the thick forest.

———————

At the door came a familiar coded knock. An old man's heavily accented voice happily answered, "My, my. Someone is at the door. Who is it, I wonder?"

"Me!" said the confident, high-pitched girl's voice from outside.

The short but well-built man scratched his bald head. "Hmm, *me*? I seem to be in here, though. You must be *you*, yes? So, *who* is you?" he asked, chuckling.

"It's *me*!" Girlish giggles followed.

The old man rubbed his short salt-and-pepper beard in pretend bewilderment. "Well, well, well…

this is quite a predicament. I seem to be both inside and outside. Hmm, I will need to think about this as I drink my coffee, yes? Goodbye, *me*."

"But you don't like coffee!" said the girl, laughing.

"I don't?" he replied. He opened the brown oak door.

"You don't! You love Tee!" A yellow blur flung itself into his strong arms. "It's so good to see you, Grandpapa!"

The old man quickly scanned outside. Satisfied, he closed the door. He put his granddaughter down and offered to take her hooded cloak, but stopped when he noticed she looked sad.

"What is it, my angel?" he asked.

She stuck her fingers through a hole in her yellow cloak, looking disappointed. "It got another one yesterday."

"Well, some say that there isn't a thing Nikolas Klaus cannot fix, and what he cannot fix, he can reinvent. I'm sure I can fix it for you." Nikolas squeezed Tee's cheeks. "Now, you'll have to tell me how this happened, because I'm sure it is an exciting story, yes?"

"It is! We built a—wait, did you make cookies?"

Nikolas feigned surprise. "Oh, I forgot—I need to

get my cookies out of the oven!"

"Cookies!" yelled Tee. She bounded up the six stairs of the split-level home and straight into the kitchen. "Chocolate chip?"

"I don't remember. I think that they are ..." and he lingered.

"What *are* they?"

"I think they are… a surprise!" He poked her nose lovingly.

Even though he'd been home alone, Nikolas was dressed in fine pants and a tailor-made shirt and vest. Over top, he wore a cooking apron. He looked like a nobleman trying very hard to dress down.

The house had exposed wooden beams and a polished wooden floor. It was unlike any house in the area—if not the entire kingdom. While packed bookshelves lined almost every wall, there were also mountains of books piled on the floor. There were few places in any kingdom, outside of royal libraries, that had as many books.

Where there weren't books there were worktables, used for drawing, set up at varying angles. Each table held ideas and inventions in differing stages of completion.

Tee sat on her favorite chair. Though Nikolas had

made many of the things in his house, he'd asked a friend to make the chair. The chair was made from a rare live tree and had grown as Tee had grown. Every time she visited, her grandfather would take it out its soil box on the deck, brush it off, and bring it in.

"Grandpapa, tell me again why your wooden floors are shiny like glass?" she asked, looking with amazement at her reflection, as she'd done for years.

Nikolas smiled and took the cookies out of the wood oven. "Now, I find it hard to believe that you came all the way over here to ask me about my floors. I've told you the story so many times. I am sure that you can explain it even better than I, now, yes?"

Tee thought about how many times she'd been over to his house—the sleepovers, the silly games, and the times they'd stayed up all night inventing things. "I suppose ..." Tee's gaze slowly moved upward, and she took a moment to appreciate the incredible detail in the kitchen's wood crown molding. "There are new parts!" remarked Tee, pointing.

"Hmm? Oh?" said Nikolas, looking at the wood trim lining the top part of the kitchen walls. "What? No. Nothing new," he said, baiting her. "It's been like that for years."

"Yes, there is." Tee stood up on her chair. "Right there. Three new symbols. You're almost out of room. I think you'll need a new board in a month or two."

Nikolas shook his head in amazement. She didn't miss much. "You are right, on both counts," he said. "But, before you ask—no."

"No, what?" asked Tee, this time baiting him.

He looked her straight in the eyes. "No, I will not tell you what it is about."

Tee had asked for years, and each time he had politely refused. He'd said it in different ways, but it was always the same result. She felt it wasn't so much that he was keeping a secret, as protecting her from its consequences. She knew that one day he would tell her—when they were both ready.

She continued looking around the kitchen while waiting for the cookies to cool. Her eyes fell upon the picture hanging above the doorway.

"I wish I could have known her," Tee said, sadness in her voice.

Nikolas turned around, holding the plate of cookies. "Who? Oh, yes, Grandmama. She would have loved you so much, my dear." His eyes welled up a bit. "Life is cruel and unfair sometimes."

After setting the cookies on the table, he got on all

fours, pushed aside a chair, and opened a trapdoor in the corner of the kitchen. "You want milk, yes, Tee?"

"Yes please, Grandpapa."

Nikolas climbed down into his small, refrigerated cellar, returning a moment later with a jug of cold milk. "So, what have you been up to that could make such a hole in your cloak?" He topped up the oversized teacup he'd been sipping all morning and then sat down with a sigh.

Tee remembered her wild ride. "Oh, yes. Well, yesterday Elly and I finished making the sail-cart, like you and I talked about."

Nikolas' eyes lit up. "Really? A sail-cart? You and your friend Elly made one? I didn't even get to show you any plans for making one yet. I just... I only told you about the idea!" He laughed with pride.

"I know, but you explained it well enough, and Elly's good with a hammer and saw."

Nikolas' face wrinkled with fatherly concern. "Isn't Elly a bit young to use a hammer?"

Tee looked at him disapprovingly for having brought up age. "She's twelve, like me, and only two inches shorter. That's plenty old enough for tools! You were younger than us when you started inventing things, anyway."

"Hmm," said Nikolas, recognizing he'd better not say anything more. His protective nature was sometimes at odds with the perhaps overly truthful stories he had shared of his own past.

"Oh, that reminds me!" Tee sprang up, bolted to the front door, went into her backpack, and returned with the red box.

"This is why I came. My dad asked me to bring you something. It arrived yesterday, and he thought you'd need it today, even though you're coming for dinner tonight. I *didn't* peek inside." Tee placed the red box on the table.

Nikolas looked at the box and sighed heavily. He smiled at Tee. "This I can look at later," he said, putting it in a kitchen drawer.

Patting her lovingly on the head, he continued, "So, tell me. What happened with your cloak and the sail-cart?"

Tee wiped her mouth on her sleeve. Her grandfather gave a disapproving look and tossed her a cloth napkin. Finished with it, she told him all about how she and Elly had spent several days making the sail-cart.

Tee continued, "Then we were going to take it up to the treehouse …"

"The secret one, high up the mountain? Isn't that a bit dangerous?" Nikolas accidentally replied.

Tee looked at him suspiciously. "How do *you* know about it?"

A couple of seconds passed, and then her grandfather tapped his right temple and smiled. "You forget that some people consider me a genius. I knew it had to be a secret because you hadn't told me about it before. You tell me everything."

Tee was unsure he was telling the whole truth, but decided to continue anyway. "We were right by Elly's house which, if you remember, is up the mountain from my house, and down the road from here."

Nikolas smiled. He knew very well where Tee's best friend lived. He'd known it since the time Tee had led him down the road, reaching way up to hold his hand, because she wanted to make sure he knew where Elly lived. She'd walked the whole way, which had taken quite some time with her little legs. When they'd arrived, she'd formally introduced him to her best friend, Elly. The memory always made him smile.

"I got in the sail-cart to show Elly that everything worked and then—"

Nikolas interrupted, "A big gust of wind! Where did you go?" He collected the dishes and started washing them in the sink.

Tee smiled awkwardly. "It kind of pushed me off the road, down the side of the mountain—toward home."

All of a sudden, this seemingly innocent, fun story had taken a serious turn. "That's when you used the brake, *yes?*" he asked, with concern.

"Well," said Tee sheepishly, "we kind of hadn't built that part yet. That was most *definitely* going to be next."

After a big sigh, and reminding himself his granddaughter was clearly okay, he chuckled and shook his head. He thought to himself that the next time he'd speak to Tee about an invention, he should discuss the safety features *first*.

"What happened then?" asked Nikolas.

Tee took a sip of milk before responding. "So, then I kind of went down the mountainside, screaming. At first, I was wondering what I was going to do. I was scared of hitting a tree, but then I realized the steering worked really well! It was so much fun."

Nikolas enjoyed her stories. He imagined Tee, in her makeshift sail-cart, going down the mountainside, heading for home. Placing the last dish in the wooden rack to dry, he turned to face Tee and leaned on the counter. With a raised left eyebrow, he said, "But the cliff... you stopped before the cliff, yes?"

Tee looked at her feet. She knew he wouldn't like this part. "Dad saved me with that crossbow bolt with the rope attached. It went through my cloak and into a tree. I was kind of stuck there for a bit."

Nikolas' eyes narrowed disapprovingly. "Where, exactly?"

Tee's head shrank into her body. "Um—in *the* tree."

"The *same* tree?" he asked in disbelief.

"Yeah." Tee slowly looked up at her grandfather.

Nikolas sat down. "Always the *same* tree. The one that is leaning off the cliff?" he said, gesturing with both hands.

Tee smiled uncomfortably. "Kind of. It's leaning more, now."

Nikolas rubbed his bald head for a moment, and then smoothed his salt-and-pepper beard. He could tell she understood this was serious and that she would've likely been killed if she hadn't been lucky. Unfortunately, she always seemed to be lucky. "Hmm, I think we need to do something for that tree. We can't have it go falling off the cliff, can we? What would save you next time?"

Tee quietly sighed in relief. "You're right. So, anyway, that's how I made the hole in my cloak." Tee felt lighter for having gotten the story off her chest.

Nikolas messed with her hair lovingly and said, "Well, I wouldn't worry about that yellow hooded cloak of yours. I—"

Suddenly, there came an unexpected, heavy-handed knocking at the door.

The three Cochon brothers walked out of the tavern, wiping the remains of lunch on their sleeves. They hadn't talked much about the morning's events. Each was embarrassed and angry.

They stopped to watch the town's people milling about. Some people were walking, some were pulling hand-carts, and some were on horses. It was like any other day. Nothing was out of the ordinary, and nothing interesting was happening—and this bothered Bakon.

Watching a pair of town guards walk by on patrol, Bakon pondered aloud, "Why would a messenger show up here? Mineau would make sense. It's a bigger town. It's easier to get to, being at the bottom of the mountain. Why come here—to Minette? We're a fraction of Mineau's size."

"Maybe he got lost?" suggested Squeals in his high-pitched, scratchy, nervous voice.

Bakon shook his head. "A man like that doesn't *get* lost. I don't think he's just a messenger, either."

Squeals asked, "Should we tell Archambault?"

Bakon shook his head again. "Not yet. We don't know anything. It's just that it doesn't make sense." He paused to watch some people load a cart before continuing. "What's so important about our town? The Magistrate isn't even back yet from wherever he went. So that means the messenger can't be expecting to see him, and that messenger is not going to deliver a message to anyone but its intended recipient."

Bore bent down and scratched the edge of his right big toe, which poked out from a loose seam in his patchwork boots. "Maybe the man's not here for the town," he said.

Bakon and Squeals turned to look at their mountain of a younger brother.

"Go on, Bore," prompted Bakon. "What are you thinking?"

Over the years, Bore had proven that while most of what he said was simple and obvious, on occasion he saw something that everyone else missed.

He pointed to the people walking around. "No

one is excited. I liked seeing him. He was fancy," said Bore, smiling. "We don't see fancy a lot."

Bakon started to laugh and slapped Bore's arm affectionately. "You're right, Bore! You are right." He smiled at the dozens of people walking around and acting like it was just an ordinary day. "People should be gossiping about him and gathering in groups. They wouldn't be like... this," he said, gesturing. "This messenger is dressed fancier than anyone in town except for *maybe* the Magistrate himself. The people wouldn't be able to help themselves."

Squeals' eyes squinted with jealousy. It was rare that Bakon ever paid him any compliments. "Well—" said Squeals, trying to think of something to earn praise, "maybe he went to see someone else!"

Bakon, disappointed, glared at Squeals. "Well of course he went to see someone else! If he's not here for the town, then he's here to deliver a message to *someone*. The question is *who* would be deserving of an almost-royal messenger?" Bakon started to march toward the center of town.

"Wait—can we go home and get our flintlocks, first?" asked Squeals, almost eating his words with nervousness. "I hate magic. If it comes again, I want to shoot it."

Bakon shook his head angrily. "There's no such thing as magic, you dimwit. How many times do I have to say it?" His brother cowered, and Bakon calmed down. "But," he continued, "I do think you finally had a good idea."

Squeals looked at the ground, and smiled.

CHAPTER THREE

HUFF AND PUFF

"Please open the door, Monsieur Klaus. This is official business. I request that you let me in," said the messenger. He knocked vigorously on the front door.

Hand to lips, Nikolas signaled his granddaughter to be quiet. When he started to move toward the kitchen's back door, Tee tugged on his sleeve.

"It's okay, Grandpapa," she whispered. "It's a man I helped earlier. He's an *official* messenger. I helped him get away from the Cochon brothers and find his horse."

Nikolas looked at Tee with surprise and concern. "I don't think you understand, my dear."

"No, Grandpapa, *you* don't understand. His name is Andre LeLoup, and he's on official business. He's nice."

Nikolas' eyes narrowed. "LeLoup?" he asked uncomfortably.

Tee nodded.

The forceful knocking came again. "I know you are inside and I require you to open the door. Now, please, let me in!" said LeLoup.

Nikolas looked at his granddaughter's pleading eyes. She didn't understand. She'd never seen him act any way except graciously toward strangers.

He knew that LeLoup's use of *official business* was his coded way of telling Nikolas that if LeLoup got what he wanted, he'd leave without anyone being harmed.

Nikolas sighed deeply, and whispered, "I need you to trust me, my dear. This is not what you think." He took her by the hand and started heading for the back door of the kitchen.

Tee slipped from his grip and ran to the front entrance. "I need my yellow cloak and backpack!" she whispered loudly.

"You have left me no choice, Monsieur Klaus!" said LeLoup angrily.

As Tee grabbed her backpack and pulled her cloak on, the door blew open with an explosive puff of smoke, knocking her against the wall and off her feet. LeLoup peered in and saw the unmoving yellow-cloaked heap on the floor.

Nikolas rushed toward LeLoup, instinctively grabbing a long plain-looking metal rod out from a hidden nook in the kitchen doorframe.

Andre LeLoup drew his flintlock pistol and pointed it at the yellow-hooded girl as she started to moan and move. He gave Nikolas a serious look that stopped him in his tracks, six feet away.

LeLoup grinned menacingly. "It is rude to keep a man waiting when he is trying to be considerate—never mind when he has been sent by Simon St. Malo."

Nikolas quickly scanned the cramped entranceway. While thinking about what to do next, he pinned the rod between his left arm and chest. He discreetly started cranking a small handle on the rod with his right hand.

"I'm surprised," said Nikolas, stalling for time, "that Simon St. Malo would send *you*."

LeLoup's face lit up. "You've heard of me?" he asked, desiring confirmation.

Nikolas nodded. "So—what does Simon want?"

LeLoup grinned again. He enjoyed playing the game of cat and mouse. "You know, you are a hard man to find. It took me weeks to track you down. I would've moved on to the next town if I hadn't encountered an extraordinary, yellow-hooded girl. I figured she might be tied to you somehow, and here we are," he said, with a hint of evil playfulness. "It would be a shame if anything were to happen to her." He gestured threateningly with his pistol.

"Congratulations, Monsieur LeLoup. You sniffed me out. Now ride back to wherever that rat is hiding and tell him the answer is *no*. Whatever his question is, the answer is *no*," said Nikolas angrily. He finished cranking the rod's handle.

LeLoup scoffed. "St. Malo knew that you wouldn't comply willingly. He asked that I get your attention by *any* means necessary and return what is rightfully his—as all inventions are. What he wants is described in *here*." LeLoup tossed a sealed envelope at Nikolas.

Without thinking, Nikolas skillfully caught the envelope. It was a simple envelope with St. Malo's seal.

"Open it," insisted LeLoup.

Nikolas opened the letter carefully. *Give me the steam engine plans and notes*, it read. Confused, he looked up. "I assure you I don't have any such plans, Monsieur LeLoup."

LeLoup rubbed his left temple. "I wasn't *planning* on shooting a young girl today, but... St. Malo knows that you've been working on it. He *wants* those plans."

For more than a year, Nikolas had been exchanging letters with his friend, Maxwell Watt, who lived in Inglea—an island kingdom to the north. It was Maxwell, and not Nikolas, who had invented the steam engine. Nikolas had only been helping Maxwell work out some of the more difficult questions that he'd been unable to solve on his own.

Simon must have a spy close to Maxwell, Nikolas thought, *but not close enough to have the full story. Perhaps a person delivering letters? Or an assistant? When did Simon get such influence as to reach across kingdoms?* He was alarmed by the idea of St. Malo getting his hands on such an invention.

LeLoup continued, "St. Malo is offering to send you an abundance of coins—*once* I have delivered the plans safely to him."

Tee carefully managed to make eye contact with Nikolas, while keeping her face turned away from LeLoup. Nikolas gave her an imperceptible nod and then sprang at LeLoup with the metal rod.

"Simple Simon has no coins!" yelled Nikolas.

When the rod's end touched LeLoup's pistol arm, electrical sparks flew everywhere. LeLoup flailed madly and fell to the ground. Throwing the rod aside, Nikolas grabbed Tee by the hand, and ran out the door.

Deep within the forest, they stopped for a moment to catch their breath. Nikolas tried to judge where they were. The strong wind was blowing leaves everywhere, making it hard to see through the trees and bushes.

"I heard something that way!" yelled an unfamiliar voice, uncomfortably nearby.

Nikolas held Tee close. "LeLoup brought other men. We must be careful," he whispered.

Tee's eyes welled up. "I'm sorry," she said quietly. "I told him I was going to your house. I shouldn't have told him. I—I—I knew he was a stranger, but he seemed nice."

Nikolas was sharply reminded that there were many things about his life he hadn't explained to her yet. He smiled reassuringly. "Shh, no crying, yes? It is not your fault. He is a master at what he does. We must be smart, and fast, yes? We will talk about this at dinner with your parents, and we will laugh. Everything will be okay."

Tee wiped her tears and nodded.

Nikolas looked around. He spotted a figure

nearby, but luckily it was heading away from them. He turned to Tee with an intense look in his dark brown eyes. "You are a smart girl. Promise me you will always be smart. Think. Don't panic. Find the strength inside you. It is there."

Tee looked at him, confused. She didn't know what he was talking about.

He checked his pockets, confirming they were disappointingly empty. "I wish I'd grabbed my coat. I had some useful items in the pockets," he muttered, and then looked around. "I need a moment to think."

Suddenly, three large men appeared out of the swirling leaves and dense underbrush. They were dressed in dark red leather armor, like the mercenary horsemen of the area.

"Go!" urged Nikolas as he pushed his granddaughter away.

CHAPTER FOUR

PACKED TOGETHER

Elly and Richy loved to hang out at the three-level treehouse. From the top floor, they could see their town of Minette on the mountain plateau below, and on clear days they could see all the way down to the much larger city of Mineau at the base of the mountain.

Some months before, Elly and Richy had been incredulous when Tee had come running up the road with a crazy story about a fantastic treehouse in the forest.

"Guys! You'll never believe what I found!" Tee had blurted out to Richy and Elly. The two had been playing cards in Richy's front yard.

Tee's cheeks were rosy and her breath was visible in the crisp spring air. Her hair and eyes were hidden by the hood of her warm yellow cloak.

Richy looked up. His messy short black hair made him appear as if he'd just woken up. He put his cards down and examined Tee. She had twigs all over her cloak. "You know—that look of *I was just running through the forest until a tree fell on me* is an interesting fashion statement, Lala."

"Yeah Lala, what's got you so excited?" asked Elly.

Elly and Lala, as they sometimes called Tee, had been friends since they were nine months old. Their mothers had met on the way to a farmer's house outside of Mineau. Since then, barely a day went by when Elly and Tee didn't see each other.

While Tee would jump into a situation without fear, Elly would always dive in after, with loyalty and faith in her friend. "You look like you ran up and then back down the mountain," Elly said.

"Well," said Tee, still huffing, "I guess I kind of did, in a way." She plunked herself down beside them. "I found something you'll never believe. There's an incredible treehouse near the top of the mountain!"

"You're right—I don't believe you," said Richy, picking his cards back up.

Elly gave Tee the eyebrow treatment. "Uh-huh. You mean the top of the mountain that we've been to at least twice a year for the past five years?"

Tee nodded.

"So," Richy said, looking at Elly and shaking his head in support, "a treehouse just magically appeared?"

Tee shook her head. "Magic? No. There's no such thing. But it did seem to appear all of a sudden. Did I mention it has three floors?"

"No way!" said Elly and Richy in unison. They laughed and looked at each other.

"Jinx!" they said in unison. Then they eyeballed each other.

"Double jinx!" they said in unison, again.

Tee waved for them to stop. "Guys! Enough jinxing. Come on! You've got to see this." Tee picked herself back up and started running up the mountain road.

"Wait!" said Richy. "We're going to need ropes and gear to get to the top of the mountain. Why are you running? It's going to take an hour or two."

"You'll see. We don't need that stuff anymore!" Tee yelled back.

———————

"Richy, what are you up to?" asked Elly from the second floor, below.

"Just thinking about the treehouse, and how weird it is that, after all this time, we're still the only ones who come here—well, other than whoever keeps adding pieces to it, and new stuff for us to find."

"I think magic elves do all that," said Elly cheekily.

"It'd be nice if they could leave some sandwiches next time. I forgot to bring a snack today." Richy looked down at the system of ropes, pulleys, and weights on the mountainside that had mysteriously appeared last spring along with the treehouse.

There were five sets of ropes to help you run up the mountain, and four sets to zip you back down to the main road that led to Minette. The system had been cleverly put together so that the ropes were hard to see from the ground, but easy to spot from the treehouse.

Richy noticed some of the weights moving, indicating someone coming up. He peered into the distance and saw a flash of yellow. "Hey, Elly! It looks like Tee's coming up. She's running crazy fast, like a bear's chasing her or something! I thought you said —"

"—that she's gone to her grandfather's house for the day, yeah." Elly climbed up the wooden stairs to join him on the third floor. "That's what her mom had said—'She won't be home until dinner. You know Tee and her Grandpapa.'" Elly tried to see what had grabbed Richy's attention.

He pointed at the flash of yellow running from rope to rope, racing up the mountain. "If she's supposed to be at her grandfather's house, then why is she running like a maniac up the mountain? She only runs that fast when she's—"

"In trouble," finished Elly, nervously. Something caught her eye further down the mountain. "Wait! What's that, Richy?"

Richy leaned over the railing and squinted. "I'm not sure. Oh—hang on. I've got an idea!" He ran down to the cabinets on the first level to get the telescope; they'd discovered it under a floorboard the week before.

Telescope in hand, Richy raced back up, oriented himself, and peered through it. After a moment, he swallowed hard.

"Elly, those are—"

———

Nikolas called out for his granddaughter again, but only the birds replied. He stepped out of the woods and onto the dusty road. He felt old and tired. Tears of worry streamed down his face.

He rubbed his bald head as he tried to think about how he was going to fix the situation. His normally calm, brilliant mind was overwhelmed by worry that Tee might be harmed. He struggled to come up with a plan.

He'd made a gross miscalculation. Andre LeLoup had been much better prepared than Nikolas had expected. Clearly, Simon St. Malo had gained more than just influence in recent years. Nikolas figured St. Malo must have found a powerful patron—someone rich enough to afford an expensive man like LeLoup plus his three horsemen.

Nikolas wondered if Simon suspected he didn't actually have the plans for the steam engine. Maybe Simon was hoping Nikolas would give up whatever he *did* have—something that could be even more valuable? Or maybe Simon was trying to show that, after all these years, he could still terrorize Nikolas?

Nikolas' thoughts returned to his granddaughter. When he'd urged Tee to run, he had assumed the horsemen would try to subdue him, and take him back to LeLoup. Instead, as soon as Tee had run off, two of them chased after her. The third one had roughed Nikolas up a bit before following the other two.

I should have known better, he kept thinking. LeLoup had given him the clue right there in his entranceway. LeLoup had said he'd do *whatever it would take* to get what he wanted—and he meant it. It was obvious now that LeLoup intended to use Tee as leverage.

Nikolas wasn't sure what to do. This had all happened so quickly, and it had been years since he'd seen any real action. Looking back now, he felt he'd allowed himself to enjoy life too much and had grown soft and slow because of it.

For too long Nikolas had thought of the Tub's battles as no longer his battles. He hung his head for a moment in recognition of how wrong he'd been. He couldn't hide from the world any longer.

Nikolas hoped he knew his granddaughter as well as he believed he did. *She should be heading to the top of the mountain,* he thought. The ropes and pulleys should allow her to stay ahead of the horsemen.

From behind, a rough voice called, "Hey! You there!"

Nikolas' shoulders slumped. He fought off the idea that LeLoup had already caught Tee—that LeLoup had already won. He wouldn't accept it unless he saw it with his own eyes.

Slowly, he turned. Three large figures walked toward him. They were about forty yards away. Two were pointing flintlock rifles at him. The shortest one, still a tall man, had a pistol in each hand, also pointing at him. The Cochon brothers!

"Look!" bellowed Bore. "It's Mister Nik. Hello Mister Nik!" Bore tossed his rifle aside carelessly, and ran to give Nikolas a huge hug.

Relief washed over Nikolas. "Boys! I'm so happy to see you." When Bore finally let him go, Nikolas fell to his knees, where he remained for a moment to catch his breath.

Bakon put his pistols away and offered a hand to help Nikolas to his feet.

Squeals shouldered his rifle. "Sorry, Mister Klaus. We didn't know it was you. What are you doing here?"

Nikolas felt a mix of emotions start to rise up inside him, with tears coming to his eyes. He steeled himself, trying to stay focused. "You ran into *the messenger* today, yes?"

Bakon's right eyebrow shot up in surprise. "Yes... How do you know that?"

Nikolas gave a sad, knowing smile. There was much he knew about what went on, about the affairs of others—a lot of which he couldn't share.

"I know there are few who come to this town without you finding out. You did try to stop him, yes?"

"Yes," said Squeals, "until Bakon was hit with magic."

"A stone! I was hit with a *stone*. It stunned me for a minute," said Bakon, irritated, subconsciously rubbing the back of his head.

"Ah, Tee. Yes, that makes sense now," muttered Nikolas to himself. Then he said aloud, "The messenger—we *must* find him."

"We'll find him eventually," said Squeals. "We didn't like his look anyway. He looked like trouble. We wanted to tell Archambault, but he's out and his guys don't listen to us."

"This man has horsemen, and"—Nicolas' voice broke—"and they are after my granddaughter." Tears started to stream down his face again.

Bakon didn't hesitate. "Which way are we going?"

CHAPTER FIVE

WENT TO MARKET

Nikolas thought back to when he had first met the Cochon brothers. It felt like a lifetime ago.

That day, he had gone to town for groceries and supplies, and noticed three very young boys waiting at the side of the road. They were just beside the wooden archway marking the southern entrance to Minette. Hours later, as he was heading home, he saw the boys were still there, still alone.

He stopped his horse and sat there on his cart, thinking. Townspeople were still milling about, but no one seemed to be paying any attention to the boys. Nikolas had seen children abandoned before, but never three at once.

Their clothes were little more than rags. Nikolas guessed they'd awoken alone at the forest's edge, and discovered that whoever had brought them here was gone. The boys had probably followed the flow of people to the entrance of town, and then planted themselves in that spot, hoping whoever it was who'd left them would return shortly.

The two younger boys, perhaps three and five years old, had tear-streaked faces. They kept looking at the ground. The eldest, not more than seven, paced about. It was obvious he was torn up inside, angry and nervous, and trying to keep his little family together.

The boys were skinny. Nikolas could see the outline of their ribs. They probably hadn't eaten properly in months. They were shoeless. Their clothing was dirty, and torn. From what he could infer from the style and fabric of their clothes, they were probably from a kingdom to the east.

Nikolas raced his horse and cart back up to the house and then started quickly unloading the supplies onto the yard. He yelled to his wife, "Isabella, I need to head back to town!"

His wife rushed out. Her husband was in a frenzy, emptying the cart so fast that he was almost throwing things out of it.

Unable to get his attention, she ran in front of him, yelling, "Wait! Wait! Nikolas! I know that look. Wait. Stop. Talk to me."

Nikolas put down the last box, and only then

realized his wife was there. "Isabella, there are three abandoned boys—and a storm is coming." His eyes told a story she knew well. She stepped out of his way.

They'd been down this road before. She knew her husband would save all the world's children if he could. But he often said that without her anchoring force, he'd be lost in the wind. She felt he needed her right now, whether he knew it or not.

Nikolas dashed into the large shed and brought back blankets, a box of wax powder, and some poles. Isabella was amazed at how he could always make his way in and out of that stuffed mess of a building as if it were actually organized; she was afraid to enter it for fear of causing an avalanche.

"Nikolas, wait—"

He quickly checked that his supplies were safely loaded onto the cart and then turned back to his wife. "Isabella—I can't. A storm's coming!" He gestured to the approaching dark gray and purple clouds. "I need to get back to those boys."

Isabella gave a compassionate smile. "Listen to me, my love," she said, stopping him with a soft touch to his face that briefly washed away his crazed look. "Your heart is as big as a mountain, but you can't save them all."

"I must save these ones. Please, Isabella." Tears welled up in his eyes.

She could see he meant it. "Okay—but let me check things first." She made sure the food he'd loaded into the cart was appropriate. She wouldn't put it past him to have accidentally taken sacks of flour instead of fruit and cheese.

Isabella gave Nikolas her nod of approval. He kissed her quickly and bounded up into the cart. "I love you with my heart, and all," he said awkwardly.

His wife waved, smiling, as her knight went off on his noble quest. As he passed out of sight, she turned toward the house. "Children, come! We have supplies to put away, and guests are coming. We need to get everything ready."

When Nikolas arrived, the boys were still at the town's entrance. He pulled his horse and cart to the opposite side of the road and onto the grass, out of the way of the people coming and going.

He climbed over and sat on the back of his cart, facing the boys. After a while, he gave them a nod of acknowledgement. The boys noticed him, but otherwise ignored him.

Experience had taught him it was too early to

engage them. He'd been in this situation before. Trust would take a little time to build.

Nikolas usually kept to himself in public, but now he made an effort to greet and chat with as many of the people he knew as they passed by. He wanted the boys to see he was friendly, and well known.

Some town guards came by and asked Nikolas what he was doing. He explained his concern, and the guards confirmed his suspicion. Early in the morning, the mother had abandoned the boys. The guards went over to the boys to explain who Nikolas was and how long they'd known his family. The boys stared at them, saying nothing.

The second hour rolled by. Nikolas unpacked some of the food. He cleaned the fruit and cut several slices of bread and cheese. He laid everything out on the cart's edge for the boys to see. He didn't offer anything yet, but he could see he had their attention.

He watched them kick a rock around for a while as they tried to keep their minds off their hunger and bleak situation.

Nikolas gestured to the sky and said to the boys, in a warm, friendly tone, "Do you see rain is coming? Those clouds will bring a hard rain, but not a long one. It will rain for a couple of hours, no more."

The boys looked at him. The eldest then looked at the sky, and back at Nikolas. "I don't see rain. You're lying—and you're trying to trick us."

Nikolas sighed. This would be harder than he'd hoped, but he could persevere. "No tricks. But maybe I see things you don't, yes? Maybe you see things I don't—and if you do, then I will learn. Maybe you'd like to learn how I see things?"

The boys looked at each other. It was clear that food was foremost on the mind of the three-year-old, but his brothers shushed him. "Why do you talk funny?" asked the eldest.

Smiling, Nikolas replied, "My wife says it is how my ideas come together from different languages—and that they get spoken all mixed up. It does not always happen. But, while there are many things I have mastered, this is not one of them."

Nikolas shrugged and continued, "I have done many things in my life, lived in many places, made many things. I grew up in one of the eastern kingdoms, which is why I have this accent."

He stood up, took a step toward the boys, and continued, "Did you know I was once like you?"

Nikolas thought back to his privileged upbringing and its harsh end when war had broken out. At the age of thirteen, he and his family had lost everything, and shortly afterward, he'd lost his family too. He'd lived by his wits for two years, learning harsh lessons —lessons which he hoped to help these boys avoid.

He pointed at the clouds again. "The rain is coming soon. Five minutes, perhaps. Time for a tent, yes? I, for one, don't like being wet." He climbed into his cart. Using the poles and blankets, Nikolas made a simple roof. He spread some of the wax dust onto the blankets, which the boys thought was quite odd.

As he finished setting up, another town guard came by. "Monsieur Klaus, there is nothing you can do here. You should go home and be with your family."

Nikolas smiled at him, saying, "Gabriel Archambault, my friend, it is always good to see you. Do you really believe that?" He beckoned the guard to look at the boys again.

Gabriel glanced at them and leaned on the cart. "Honestly? It's amazing you don't give up. We've known each other a few years now. You've tried this twice before, with no success. I think of you like an older brother, so I'll say what I mean. You, of all people, have better things to do."

Nikolas shook his head. "Ah. Like making such

things to help my friends involved in their secret affairs?"

Gabriel was a bit taken aback by Nikolas' frankness.

"You suspected, yes?" said Nikolas. He smiled, letting his friend off the hook. He scratched his short dark beard and ran a hand through his thinning brown hair. "Helping a society starts with its children. If these boys can be taught how to help society—or if they can simply be taught how to *harm it less* than is their nature—then it is worth it. It is rare that we have an opportunity to shape society at such a pivotal point, yes? Anyway—my time and energy are mine to lose."

Guardsman Archambault sighed, stroked his bushy mustache, and looked at Nikolas. "You're a better man than me. I don't know where your drive comes from. I hope"—Gabriel paused, wondering—"I hope someday I have kids, and that you're there to advise me."

Nikolas smiled. "I hope so too, but if I'm not, remember— rules are fine to guide you, but not to keep us from doing the right thing."

The rain started. "Oh! It appears my time has run out," exclaimed Nikolas.

Gabriel walked over to the boys, and then bent down to eye level with the eldest. "You have no idea who this man is, and what he is going to offer you. He's a saint. Take Monsieur Klaus up on the offer. You only get one chance like this in life." Having said that, Gabriel felt lighter. He wondered if there was some truth in what Nikolas had said.

He stood up and waved at Nikolas. "Good luck."

Nikolas nodded, and returned the wave as Gabriel resumed his patrol.

The boys huddled under a tree, trying to stay out of the cold summer rain as it came down faster and faster.

Nikolas spoke loudly, to overcome the rain's roar. "You know, I spread wax dust on the blankets to make the rain slide off. I have a friend—she is a master of candles—and she taught me the trick."

He turned, looking at his handiwork, but then pointed out a few leaks. "Still, it is not perfect. Many things in this life, they are not perfect, but we must seize the opportunity to try and make them better, yes?"

The boys looked at Nikolas, bewildered.

"Am I speaking too funny? Maybe some food will help you understand me," he said.

The boys came over to the cart. They looked at the food, but stood there, uncertain.

After a minute, in a squeaky, small voice, the middle brother asked, "May I please have some food?"

"Of course, you may," said Nikolas gently. He then lifted the boy up and onto the cart. "Take what you like."

Nikolas looked at the youngest one next, who was nearly as tall as his middle brother. "You, I think, like apples, yes?" He handed one to the boy.

"Oh, yes," replied the husky, little voice. Nikolas reached down and lifted him onto the cart. "You *are* a big boy!" he said, surprised at his weight. "Do you eat rocks?"

"No," said the boy, giggling. He then bit into the apple.

Finally, Nikolas turned to the eldest, who was staring at the ground. Nikolas paused, thinking back to how he'd felt when a hand had been extended to him, long ago.

"I learned a hard lesson once," said Nikolas in a serious but warm tone. "It is not weakness to accept help when one needs it. It is strength. Do you believe this?"

For a moment, the eldest boy just stood there. He looked up at Nikolas. Tears were in his eyes. Nikolas smiled the same compassionate smile his wife had given him. "You have taken good care of your brothers. I do not want to take that from you. You will continue this, but my family and I will help you. I lost my family once and a stranger helped me. Now, let me help you."

The eldest boy started to tremble. Emotion and tears streamed out. The boy threw himself into Nikolas' arms. Nikolas lifted him onto the cart to join his brothers. "I heard her say she was going to do this," he sobbed. "I heard her—and I couldn't stop her."

The younger boys burst into tears. Nikolas pulled them into a hug as tears rolled down his own cheeks.

CHAPTER SIX

TRICKY PREY

Richy nearly dropped the telescope. "There are men on horses! And smoke! I think—I think they have guns!"

Elly started jumping up and down—a nervous habit she'd had since she was little. "Um, um, um," she repeated. After a moment, her eyes lit up and she grounded herself. "Okay—I know what we're going to do."

She raced downstairs to the wall of cabinets. Opening one particular empty cabinet, she knocked out its secret back panel and grabbed one of the three pairs of dull-gray metal rods. The rods were each a foot and a half long, with a small handle near one end.

"I've got my *sticks*. I'm going down to get her!" Elly said, furiously cranking one of the handles.

Elly had discovered the sticks a month before. Unlike her fellow Yellow Hoods, Elly had a natural feel for the sticks, and had quickly figured out how to use them effectively. The sticks felt solid and perfectly balanced in her hands—neither too heavy, nor too light. She practiced with them every day.

"You're planning on going down there?!" Richy's deep blue, almond-shaped eyes were open wide. "That's crazy! What am I supposed to do—stay here and watch you both get shot or run down?" He was freaking out and breathing fast.

Elly was concerned Richy might pass out if she didn't do something; he'd passed out once before. She looked at Richy and said slowly and sincerely, while stroking his tousled hair, "Richy, we need you. I need you."

Richy started to calm down. "But... we're just *kids*."

For a moment, Elly felt like that simply stated truth might erase her own courage. "No, Richy— we're not. We *were* kids.

"Just think of that game we always play. The one where we pretend someone is chasing one of us, and the rest of us must come to the rescue."

Finished with her first stick, Elly started cranking the second, while keeping her brown eyes locked on Richy.

"Um... okay." Richy seemed to be accepting the

idea.

"Your *mission*, Richy, is to find some town guards. Bring them to Tee's grandfather's house, okay? We're going to save her. You're going to be a hero. We've done this a million times before."

Richy took a breath and nodded. "I know, but—" he said, starting to panic again.

"We'll be okay. I promise." Elly gave him a light-hearted wink and smile. She wished she felt as confident as she sounded.

With a final sigh, Richy said, "Okay—get help. Go to Tee's grandfather's house. Got it. Wait... why *his* house?"

"Because when Tee's the one playing the hunted kid, that's where she pretends to go." Elly then deftly placed both charged shock-sticks into her homemade yellow cloak's special pockets and then flipped up her hood.

"This'll all work out. I promised, remember?" said Elly. She dashed out of the treehouse, grabbed the wooden handlebar of the pulley system, and started flying down the mountain.

Richy nodded to reassure himself. "I can do this. Elly's going to distract the horsemen and not get killed.

"Everyone is going to be fine," he repeated to himself before finally racing off at top speed in search of the town guards.

Tee stumbled as she stepped away from the second-to-last pulley leading up the mountain. She was exhausted and starting to worry she wasn't going to make it. Even if she did, she didn't know what she'd do when she got there.

LeLoup's three horsemen were having some trouble getting up the steep mountainside, but they were slowly gaining on her. They had fired their flintlock pistols in hopes of scaring Tee into stopping —and she almost had.

Tee tripped and fell. She lay there, unable to find the energy to get up again, until she heard the familiar zipping sounds of pulley, weights, and ropes.

"Lala! Lala!" came a heart-warming yell from Elly.

Tee picked herself up. Her eyes welled up as she saw Elly flying down toward her, in her own yellow hooded cloak.

Elly landed and with a quick look and nod, and Tee instinctively knew what Elly had in mind. While Elly was shorter than Tee by a couple of inches, and had fairer hair, both expected the horsemen wouldn't notice the difference.

"Richy's gone for help. Go to your grandfather's house," said Elly quickly and decisively.

As she started to head out, Tee grabbed her. "Use my cloak. They might realize the color's not quite the same." She handed Elly her cloak, keeping hold of her slingshot. Elly slipped her sticks into Tee's cloak and then pulled it on.

Elly then set off down the mountain at top speed. As she approached the first horseman, she pulled out one of her sticks, pressed its activation button, and threw the stick at him.

Sparks flew as the stick connected with the rider. He flailed and fell off his horse. Elly's second stick missed the next rider. As she passed the two remaining horsemen, they turned to pursue her.

They took the bait, thought Tee. She lay on the ground, breathing heavily. She knew she had about two minutes before the pulley system reset.

Tee imagined for a moment that the treehouse and its incredible pulley system had been the work of mysterious little elves. It was a ridiculous idea, but that silly, little-kid thought made her feel better.

Then, with a familiar wooden clonk, Tee knew the pulley system was ready. She sprang up and headed back down the mountain.

The Cochon brothers tried to keep up with Nikolas as he moved through the thick forest with renewed energy and drive. He had abandoned his old-man demeanor. For a man in his late-fifties, he actually could put most of the town guards to shame.

All of a sudden, Nikolas stopped and put a finger to his lips. "Do you hear that?" he whispered.

The brothers listened for a moment.

Squeals shook his head.

Bakon and Bore looked around.

"Wait—I hear something," whispered Squeals.

Nikolas looked up to the trees. "One of the pulleys! Someone's coming down—and fast."

The brothers looked at each other, confused. They looked up and around, but couldn't see anything.

Then something zipped by overhead. "Big yellow bird!" yelled Bore, pointing.

"That's no bird—that's a yellow-cloaked kid. Get the kid, Bore!" commanded Bakon.

Bore tore off into the forest, with his eyes narrowed and his head down.

Nikolas appeared startled at Bore's sprint. The brothers smiled knowingly.

Bakon chuckled. "He'll get her, no worries about it," he said, slapping Nikolas on the shoulder. "That brother never fails."

A minute later, following the tunnel of broken branches and bushes that Bore had left in his wake, they found him singing and dancing around with Tee on his shoulders. She was singing along, enjoying the ride. Bore looked surprised to see them, having been lost in the moment.

Tee acrobatically leapt off Bore's shoulders, landing expertly. "La-la!" she exclaimed triumphantly.

Nikolas smiled in relief. "Tee! I'm so happy you're okay. But I am surprised. You were not frightened by my big friend?"

Tee shrugged. "I guess there are parts of your life I don't know." She turned to look at Bakon. "Um— sorry for hitting you with my slingshot. I... ah— sorry," she finished awkwardly.

Bakon smiled in response. "Ah, so it *was* you. That explains it. One day we'll talk about it, but not now."

"Also, Grandpapa, Bore didn't give me enough time to be scared. Before I knew it, he picked me up onto his shoulders and started singing *Mister Nik is going to be so happy*. I joined in, and he started dancing."

Something caught Nikolas' eye. He examined Tee's cloak. "This isn't yours?"

Tee suddenly remembered. "Elly!"

Andre LeLoup was frustrated. When his men had gone after Klaus and his granddaughter, he had returned to the house to search for the steam engine plans.

Simon St. Malo had told him to expect to find the plans in a long brass tube or on one of the worktables. He'd figured they should be easy to find. That hadn't been the case.

LeLoup kicked over a pile of books. "This place is such a mess! How does he find anything here?" He tried angrily to overturn one of the worktables, only to discover it was bolted down.

After calming down, he rummaged through every cabinet, every drawer, and examined every scrap of paper he could find. He stared angrily at the stupid little red box on the floor in the middle of the mess. He wanted to stomp it flat.

Not only had he found nothing regarding a steam engine, he hadn't found anything that could serve as a potential substitute to appease St. Malo.

He started to wonder if this guy really was the

famous, inventive genius behind the Tub? Maybe he was a fraud? Klaus' life seemed too simple and mundane. To LeLoup, it was almost offensive.

He decided he needed a break—to make a cup of tea, and reflect. At least he could appreciate Klaus' selection of tea. After making a cup, he sat down and gazed around the small kitchen. It was so… *common* that it was almost painful to look at.

LeLoup was one of the whispered names in the western kingdoms. He was known to get you what you wanted—whether a message delivered, or an item acquired. He avoided assassination work; it lacked a certain amount of class, in his opinion.

He wasn't yet the most infamous 'messenger' in the profession, but he wanted to be. He had only ever failed once, and though it had happened very early in his twenty-year career, it still haunted him. If he didn't return with what St. Malo had asked for, or better, his career would be over.

Simon St. Malo had offered him three times his usual fee—a great amount of money—to get some drawings from an old man. That amount had made Andre suspicious, so he had done some research on Klaus and St. Malo. He'd learned about a rivalry that stretched back decades. St. Malo seemed to make it his business to take and twist whatever Klaus invented. Though St. Malo was also an inventor, he was nothing compared to Klaus. In fact, St. Malo seemed to be insanely jealous of the man's pure genius.

LeLoup picked up and played with the long shocking rod, but couldn't get it to work. He cast it aside, deciding it was not worth bringing to St. Malo. How could it possibly compare with something called a *steam engine*? St. Malo had made it clear: The steam engine would radically change the movement of people, soldiers, and weapons. A *stick* wasn't going to satisfy him.

Andre's eyes wandered up to the kitchen ceiling. He appreciated quality woodworking, and noticed the intricate crown molding. The five-inch tall strip of wood had the most detailed set of engraved symbols and shapes he'd ever seen.

As Andre relaxed, he started to wonder if it wasn't just for decoration. He slowly got up and toured the other rooms. As he exited each room, he became more and more convinced that the kitchen's moldings were indeed out of place.

"You, my curious woodwork, are only in here. Why is that? I'm certain Klaus likes to sit here, as I do, sipping his tea. Which means—you must be hiding a story. Are you related to the plans, I wonder? Maybe something better?" he pondered aloud.

Andre stood up on a chair to get a better view. "What are you trying to say, hmm? My ears can almost hear your story. My nose can smell the importance. But, I can't see you properly, my curious woodwork. There isn't enough light," he said.

He paused for a moment, letting a thought from the depths of his mind bubble up. "Enough light," he muttered to himself.

He hopped off the chair and went back to the entrance of the home. He looked at the stairs leading from the entranceway landing up to the kitchen, and the walls on either side. Something didn't seem quite right.

Opening the front door, he looked again at the stairs and the walls on either side. Picking up a shoe, he threw it to the left of the stairs and watched it bounce off the wall. Then he threw a shoe to the right of it, and watched it go through what looked like a wall and land on an unseen floor below. The house was a split-level.

"Ah—a *trompe-l'oeil*," he said, smiling from ear to ear. "Smart, Klaus. An illusion painted so perfectly, you can't see the stairs that go down. You didn't account for the lighting at this exact time of day, did you? No—how could even you account for everything?" said LeLoup, feeling superior for the first time in a while.

He carefully went down the hidden stairs, through a short corridor, and came to a closed door with light pouring out from under it. He opened the door and stepped into a large room.

There were wall-to-wall bookcases in the room, but unlike upstairs, there were neither worktables nor books on the floor. In front of an empty fireplace was a nice rug, and on that, a comfortable-looking, worn couch and a disused, worn decorative chair and ottoman.

Andre did a full tour, hunting again for a brass tube or plans. There was nothing—nothing but books, bookcases, a fireplace, furniture, and the rug.

"So, is this room as simple as it seems? I doubt it. Why have the stairs painted so perfectly to look like a wall? Every time I take you for simple, Monsieur Klaus, you show me I'm wrong."

He examined a dozen books, one by one, and discarded each of them. He moved the furniture and rolled up the rug. There were some meaningless lines;

clearly the hardwood flooring had been imperfectly done.

Then something dawned on him. There were no windows, no oil lamps, nor any candles—and yet the room was perfectly lit. Bewildered, Andre walked into the middle of the room and held out his arm to see where the shadow would be cast.

"No shadows? Remarkable. So, this man *is* a genius. A master of hiding in plain sight, it seems."

"LeLoup!" came a faint shout from one of his horsemen outside. Andre ran out to join them.

Two of his men were standing beside their horses. A yellow bundle was tied up beside them, on the ground.

"Only two of you? Where's the other one?" he demanded to know.

"He didn't make it," said one of the horsemen.

"What? Taken down by a girl in a yellow hood?" said LeLoup aghast.

"Um, yes," said the other horseman.

"Well," said LeLoup, "it seems that a Klaus of any age isn't to be underestimated."

"We did catch her though!" said the first horseman, pointing at the yellow bundle.

Andre rolled his eyes. "Yes. I can *see* that." He

couldn't see her face, but didn't care.

"Excellent. Things are getting back on track," said Andre. "Put her in the kitchen. Monsieur Klaus will come to us now." He couldn't help but grin.

CHAPTER SEVEN
WHAT BIG EARS

Egelina-Marie's mother had wanted her to have a different career—anything other than being one of the guards*men*. She wasn't sure how she'd tell her friends that her only child, her lovely daughter, had become a town guard.

"Egg-lean-na Mar-ie" her mother would say, drawing out her name, believing it would help her daughter change her mind. "What type of career is that for a woman? You could be a seamstress, or a nurse, or—"

"A guardsman, Mama. I want to be a guardsman, like Papa," Egelina-Marie would reply.

A couple of months ago, when her daughter had turned nineteen years old, she finally accepted the path her daughter had chosen.

She'd been coming to terms with it over time— ever since she'd first noticed her daughter sneaking off into the forest with an old rifle of her father's.

Sometimes she would secretly follow her daughter and watch her practice, amazed at her skill as she shot, from an incredible distance away, at rocks she'd lined up on a fallen tree.

Yesterday, as she'd watched her daughter up on stage with the other boot camp graduates, her heart had filled with pride. Egelina-Marie was the only woman among them, and from the reaction of the crowd, she wouldn't be the last. Her mother admired her daughter's determination—it reminded her so much of her husband.

———————

"You *must* remember," said the overbearing sergeant to Egelina-Marie, "that even when you are marching for hours, you have to stay alert. It's probably the most important lesson for day one. You never know when *something* is going to happen. You need to be ready for it."

Egelina-Marie rolled her eyes and kept walking. They had already talked about alertness and being ready for anything. It had been repeated many times over at the month-long boot camp. It had been emphasized almost to the exclusion of everything else, other than basic fighting skills and—of course — the importance of not shooting yourself or a colleague.

The sergeant could sense Egelina-Marie's irritation. "You don't believe me?" he asked, puffing up his chest.

She stopped and turned to look at him. "Look where we are. We are on a mountain road in the middle of nowhere, surrounded by forest. This place has no political importance. It doesn't have any resources. All it has is a great view, nice people, and —"

The sergeant interrupted and smugly stated, "Cheese. Everyone loves our cheese. It is the heart of the commerce of our town." He rubbed his belly unconsciously.

Egelina-Marie laughed. "Will we be invaded for our cheese, then? I'll keep my eyes peeled for giant mice."

The sergeant shook his head. He didn't appreciate her attitude. "Danger and surprise can come in all forms. There are bears and—"

Egelina-Marie turned and started walking again. "Okay, bears. Mountain lions. Sometimes, even bandits," she said, agreeing there was some danger to be found.

The sergeant was about to say something else, but Egelina-Marie quickly gestured for him to stop and be quiet.

"What? Now there's suddenly danger? Are you making fun of me?" he asked.

"Look!" She pointed to a boy, far off in the distance, running up the road and waving his arms.

The sergeant looked around. "What?" he said. He took his rifle from his shoulder.

"Don't you see him?" said Egelina-Marie, surprised at her companion. "Right there! A young boy, running up the road, yelling something. I can't read his lips but I can tell something is wrong." She started to run.

"What boy? Hey! Where are you going?"

Richy kept waving at Egelina-Marie until he was certain she was coming. He had started to believe this would be the first day in his life he wouldn't run into guards on patrol.

"I need your help! You have to go to Monsieur Klaus' house!" repeated Richy, gasping.

Egelina-Marie examined the boy. Confirming he wasn't visibly injured, she said, "Slowly, please. What's the problem?"

Richy nodded as he reorganized his thoughts. "You have to help. My friend is in trouble. There are men on horses, with guns, and they're chasing her!"

"Okay, enough!" said the sergeant, huffing and puffing as he finally arrived. "Move along, troublemaker."

Egelina-Marie was taken aback. "He was telling me there are men on horses, with guns."

The sergeant looked down at Richy. "Hmm—not likely. You can't trust children." He almost spat the last word out.

"I'm thirteen!" said Richy, offended. He straightened up to his full height. Though he was gangly, he was the tallest of the Yellow Hoods, and came up to the sergeant's shoulder and Egelina-Marie's chin.

"They're always coming up with stories like this. They want to see us dance like puppets, while they pull the strings," said the sergeant. "Bah! You'll come to learn they can't be trusted."

Richy knew kids who had done exactly that, sometimes finding themselves marched off for a visit to the town jail. "No, not me! I've never done that!" said Richy. "You don't even know me! Please!" Richy was starting to panic.

The sergeant scoffed. "You're all alike. *Troublemakers!* Now go!"

Egelina-Marie threw a sharp look at the sergeant.

"Didn't you say we needed to be alert?"

"This is not what I meant," her superior replied defensively.

Trying to prove his point, the sergeant asked, "Did you see a bear?"

"No," Richy replied, puzzled. He didn't see what this had to do with the situation.

"Did you see, perhaps, a mountain lion?" The sergeant was being patronizing.

"No, but—" Richy tried to reply.

"Leave, before we arrest you." The sergeant gestured for him to leave.

Egelina-Marie glared at the sergeant. "I'm going with him. I believe him."

"No, you are not," said the sergeant. "My orders to you are to continue the patrol."

Richy looked at Egelina-Marie with hope, and then tugged on her hand. "Please—quickly. My friends are in trouble. Monsieur Klaus is in trouble."

When she turned to run off with Richy, the sergeant raised his rifle and took aim.

"Stop!" he barked at them. "You are under arrest! This is your last chance. As a guardsman, you are to follow orders from your superior. Leave the boy, and come back here, now! Or else... or else I will be forced to shoot."

Egelina-Marie couldn't believe the irony of the situation, given their earlier conversation. She slowed and hollered back, "I doubt you can even see us properly from there. Shoot if you have to—I have people to save."

Tee stamped her foot and looked at her grandfather with steely eyes. "I won't!"

Bakon interrupted, "It's for your own good, kid."

Tee was frustrated and angry. There was no way she'd abandon Elly. "I'm *not* going home. She's my best friend. She's in danger because she saved me!"

Nikolas bowed his head to think. He was stuck between his granddaughter's loyalty to her friend, and his sense of duty to her and her mother. He couldn't argue with how she felt—after all, he'd been secretly building it up in her for quite some time.

"Squeals' back," said Bakon. Squeals emerged from the bushes, brushing needles and dirt off his shirt.

Everyone gathered around to hear Squeals' report. "I was able to get a look into the kitchen. There's a yellow-cloaked kid in there. She's doing a good job of keeping her face hidden. I think LeLoup might not know he has the wrong kid." He gave a hopeful smile.

Nikolas stroked his beard. "Yes. This changes a few things," he mused. "Some very important things." He turned to Tee. "My dear, are you sure you are ready for this?"

"Yes!" she said determinedly.

"Good. We are going to need you if we are going to throw LeLoup off his game," said Nikolas thoughtfully.

Tee pulled her slingshot from one of Elly's cloak pockets. "I'm ready."

Her grandfather smiled. "Good. This is what we will do." He started to outline his plan to the group.

Tee's thoughts returned to Elly. *I won't let you down*, she promised herself.

CHAPTER EIGHT

WHAT SHARP TEETH

Nikolas walked down the road toward his house. The mounted horseman at the front of the house kept an eye trained on him as he slowly approached. When Nikolas was about a hundred yards away, the horseman raised his flintlock pistol.

"Tell LeLoup," said Nikolas, projecting his voice, "that I want to talk with him, if you'd be so kind."

As a precaution, the horseman scanned the forest on either side of the road. Convinced Nikolas was alone, the horseman called into the house for LeLoup.

LeLoup came to the doorstep. He held Klaus' long shocking rod in one hand, and straightened his mustache with the other.

"Monsieur Klaus, of everything in your home, this is the most interesting thing I've found—and yet, it is not very interesting." He omitted the fact that it was the only thing he'd found of any note. "I've never been so quickly disarmed. This small handle seems clunky, inelegant. It's a shame it's now broken," said LeLoup, arrogantly assuming that was the reason he couldn't get it to work.

Nikolas took his time answering. "I can see clearly from here that it isn't broken. I'm quite surprised you can't figure it out. A man of your reputation should be able to handle such a simple device, yes? Even a *child* can use it." He didn't like to be patronizing, but he could see it bothered LeLoup and he needed every advantage he could get right now. Nikolas guessed LeLoup was insecure underneath his bravado. "Could you hand it over?" he said, gesturing to LeLoup. "I'll demonstrate. It really couldn't be *more* simple."

LeLoup bit his lip, trying to think of a witty response that wouldn't make him look weak. He walked out of the house, and up to the horseman who still had a pistol trained on Nikolas.

Turning to Nikolas, and sporting a false smile, LeLoup said, "No, I don't believe you could get it to work either. I'm sure it is a single-use thing, its mysteries now consumed. But... do you know what still has value? Your granddaughter's life. I have *her*. You have what I want. A trade is in order."

Nikolas feigned surprise and dismay. "Oh my! You have her, do you? I don't believe you."

"Why else would you be here?" asked LeLoup, feeling smug at having the advantage. "You will give me what I want if you want your grand—"

Before he could finish, Tee stepped out from behind Nikolas. Her hood was drawn back so that LeLoup could clearly see her face.

LeLoup recoiled in shock. "What! Is this a trick? I have her tied up in the kitchen!" He shot an angry glare at the horseman beside him, who shrank back and shrugged his shoulders.

"Nope. I'm right here!" gloated Tee.

Nikolas could see something in LeLoup had become unhinged. "It is time to put a stop to all of this, LeLoup."

"No! I don't believe you! Nice try, Klaus," barked LeLoup.

Tee took a confident stance. "I can only imagine how your reputation will be damaged by having been bested by the *little girl* in a yellow hood. It might be worse than having been saved by that same little girl, I'm sure. Maybe you should just tell people you were beaten by *The Yellow Hoods*? That might sting less."

"I didn't need your help!" growled LeLoup. "I

could have dealt with those hooligans!"

"Oh, I'm sure you could have," said Tee, patronizingly. "There, on your knees, at the mercy of those Cochon boys. Tsk."

LeLoup's face reddened with rage. This was supposed to have been an easy in-and-out mission. Instead, it was coming apart. He hated when things got messy.

He'd always figured the stories he'd heard about the Tub were exaggerations—tales made up and spread by its members for their own glory. Now he feared becoming another one of those stories.

LeLoup twitched in frustration, the humiliation seeping into his soul like a toxin. "Wait here!" he yelled at Nikolas and Tee. "And you," he barked to his horseman, "if they move—shoot them." He marched back into the house.

As he went up the stairs to the kitchen, he glanced through the back window and saw his other horseman guarding the rear of the house. "At least *someone* is doing what they're supposed to," he grumbled. He looked at the yellow-cloaked lump in the middle of the kitchen—it was larger than he remembered.

"Why are there two yellow cloaks in this pile?" he

muttered to himself. He knelt down and yanked on one of them, yelling, "Let me see your face!"

"Hello Mister Wolf!" said Bore, smiling.

"What?!" screamed LeLoup, jumping backward against a wall. His pistol, unbeknownst to him, fell out of his belt.

Meanwhile, outside, Squeals signaled to Nikolas from the forest.

"They've rescued Elly," whispered Nikolas to Tee. Her face immediately lit up.

Back in the house, something caught LeLoup's eye. He looked out the back window just in time to see another familiar ruffian surprise his horseman and tackle him to the ground.

"This is not happening!" LeLoup screamed as he ran for the front door.

"It's over. You've lost," said Nikolas to LeLoup as he emerged. "Let this end now." He was hopeful, but not overconfident. Nikolas had been in situations before where the tables had turned at the last second.

Squeals came forward from the forest's edge, his pistol pointing at LeLoup. Bore exited the house and joined his brother. LeLoup could see, from the corner of his eye, Bakon coming around the house behind him, having dealt with the horseman at the back.

Tee ran off to join Elly behind some bushes.

LeLoup's horseman slowly dropped his pistol, dismounted his horse, and put his hands in the air.

LeLoup glared at the man in disbelief. "What are you doing, fool?"

The horseman looked back and forth between LeLoup and the Cochon brothers, who were closing in. "I am not going to die," he replied.

"Leave," commanded Bakon to the horseman. "Never come back to this town."

The horseman turned and started to run. LeLoup grabbed for his pistol only to realize that he'd lost it. Spotting the horseman's gun on the ground, LeLoup dove, grabbed it, and fired.

As the horseman fell to the ground, LeLoup threw something into the air, covered his head, and closed his eyes.

Tee and Elly heard a loud boom and the sound of a terrified horse running off. The clearing in front of the house was filled with smoke and dust.

"What happened?" shouted Elly, her ears ringing. "Are they... are they dead?"

Tee tried to detect any signs of life. There was only dusty silence. Frantic with worry, she turned to Elly. "They can't be."

The smoke cleared a little. Someone stood in the middle of the clearing. A deep, dark laughter pierced the air.

"There!" said Tee, hopefully.

"Hahahaha. Oh my!" said LeLoup with triumphant joy. "You almost had me. I have to admit... what a good job you did getting under my skin! All those stories I'd heard about the Tub ...When the stories of this day spread, everyone will come to know that you're just like everyone else, and that Andre LeLoup disproved the legends. Well played, though. You had almost won.

"But you thought yourself smarter than you are, Monsieur Klaus. You may be an inventor of sorts— and a member of the Tub—but you are nothing compared to me. I am a master of getting things done," said LeLoup triumphantly.

Bore, Bakon, and Squeals had been blown backward and lost their weapons, having taken the brunt of the explosion. Nikolas was on his hands and knees in the dirt, still stunned by the blast.

The girls saw LeLoup standing over him, slowly taking out the supplies he needed to reload his pistol. LeLoup was enjoying the moment and taking his time.

"We've got to do something," said Tee, looking around. The ringing in her ears was fading. "We don't have long. What can we do?"

"Um, um, um" said Elly, bouncing up and down nervously. "Should we run out there?"

"No," said Tee. "My grandfather would never forgive me. We've got to be smart." Tee grabbed her slingshot. "Elly, find me a stone? It's got to be—"

"I know the size," she answered, scrambling. "Isn't that an impossible distance?"

"We'll find out," said Tee, trying to block the panic that was building up inside of her.

Bore clutched the ground as if it would stop the dizziness. He looked over at Squeals, who was knocked out cold. Bakon, nearby, was fighting hard to recover. His face had a blind determination on it that brought Bore back to the moment when the brothers had been abandoned, and Bakon had promised them that they'd be fine.

LeLoup finished reloading the pistol and tucked it into his belt. He then crouched down and playfully looked into Klaus's eyes. "You know that little *boom* I made, old man? I invented it. Well—I stole some parts from a man of no consequence and made it better. I gave it more force! But the real beauty is in the sound it makes. That ringing in your ears—the feeling of your head spinning? That's the masterpiece. I hope you *appreciate* it."

Reaching into his own ear, LeLoup pulled out some tightly wrapped cotton. "But that beauty is easily defeated, if you know how. Otherwise, *this"*— he gestured at Nikolas—"happens to you. Now, where were we?" He stood up and grabbed the pistol from his belt.

"I can't find a good one!" said Elly. "How can there not be a single smooth stone?"

"Keep looking! There's got to be one. It can't end like this!" said Tee, feeling around furiously on the forest floor.

LeLoup looked up for a moment, unsure if he'd heard something from the bushes. Shrugging off the distraction, he waited for Nikolas to respond. He needed to hear the defeat in the old man's voice.

Bakon staggered to his feet and bent over, placing his hands on his knees. He was shaking his head to try and clear the ringing and the last of the dizziness.

Nikolas, meanwhile, turned his head up and looked LeLoup in the eyes. He could barely hear LeLoup, but he could read his face and lips enough to understand what LeLoup was saying. Like the others, Nikolas' head was spinning.

"Well?" asked LeLoup, licking his lips and relishing the moment.

Nikolas glanced around. The girls were safe. Bakon was dealing with the effects of the blast, but clearly couldn't be of any help. Squeals and Bore were not in good shape.

He hoped LeLoup was enough of a professional that if everything were over with quickly, he'd immediately leave and Nikolas' family and friends would be unharmed. Nikolas bowed his head and quietly said, "Whatever you want—the answer is still *no*."

"If I can't get what St. Malo wants," said LeLoup, teeth clenched, "then at least I'll have *this*."

"I've got one!" yelled Elly, tossing the stone to Tee, who snatched it out of the air.

Bakon was finally over the last effects of the explosion. He charged at LeLoup.

Tee pulled back on her slingshot.

A gunshot rang out.

CHAPTER NINE

WHAT KEEN EYES

Captain Gabriel Archambault marched into the hospital and down the hallways until he came to a white door with two guards outside. He nodded to them as he opened the door and entered the room.

Over many years, his desire for adventure and action had been replaced with acceptance of a much more mundane world. Time had traded his slim, muscular body for a fat belly, a big bald spot, and a bit of a hunch. Even his gray mustache seemed to have gained weight.

The room was crowded and noisy. "Who are all these people?" yelled an annoyed Gabriel to everyone. "All of you! If you don't have to be here at this moment, get out!"

Everyone stopped in surprise and looked at him. Most of them immediately left. Three guards, a doctor, and a nurse remained.

"What's the story?" Gabriel asked them, annoyed

that he'd had to come all the way down to the hospital to find out. It had already been a long day, and the last thing he wanted was to spend time in the *house of sick people*, as he often called it.

A sergeant stepped forward. "Captain Archambault," he said, saluting.

Captain Archambault tried not to roll his eyes at the salute; he was not in a patient mood. "Did we get LeLoup?" he asked hopefully.

"LeLoup is over there, sir," answered the sergeant, pointing to a hospital bed partially obscured by the doctor and nurse. "He's not going anywhere, sir."

Gabriel glanced over at the two occupied hospital beds.

The sergeant continued, "He took a pretty serious pounding from one of those Cochon brothers."

"Are we laying charges?" asked Gabriel, concerned. He wondered if he would have to reveal his relationship with the brothers.

"I wasn't planning on it, sir," said the sergeant, shaking his head.

"Good. But I think you need to correct your wording. If someone were to assault someone else in this town, they would *have to* be charged. However, if someone *fell* on someone else, that would be a simple accident. So—are you saying that the Cochon brother *fell* on Monsieur LeLoup?"

"Yes, sir," said the sergeant, nodding to the new version of events. "He fell."

"How unfortunate for Monsieur LeLoup. What about the other one?" asked Gabriel, nodding toward the second bed.

"He died a half hour ago. Shot by LeLoup at close range. There was nothing we could do for him, sir."

The captain rubbed his chin. "Any witnesses?"

The sergeant straightened up proudly. "We have many witnesses. The victim also lived long enough to tell me what happened. I'd arrived on the scene first, along with one of our graduates."

The captain nodded approvingly. "Okay," he said, unfolding his arms and looking around. "Why are there still a doctor and a nurse here? This man died, and LeLoup just suffered injuries caused by someone falling on him."

A young woman in guard uniform stepped forward and saluted the captain. "Sir, that's because they just removed the bullet from LeLoup's shoulder. I shot him before he took the pounding from Monsieur Cochon."

The sergeant stepped between the woman and the

surprised captain. "Sir, allow me to introduce one of our newest graduates. She only started this morning and has already started making a name for herself. Her name is Egelina-Marie... ah... Archambault."

The captain glared at the sergeant. "Really? I know I look old, but do you think me a stupid old man who can't recognize his own daughter?"

"Ah, s-s-sorry sir," stammered the sergeant.

Gabriel rolled his eyes before looking at his daughter. "Hello, love."

"Captain!" she replied professionally.

Gabriel looked at the floor and mentally kicked himself. He'd done exactly what he'd told her not to do. Many times he'd said: *You can't call me Papa when you are on duty. You will need to call me Captain. I will be calling you by your rank or last name or both—the same as I do with everyone else.*

Yet here he was, the first time he ran into her, and he'd failed to follow his own advice. He thought back to an old conversation with Nikolas about rules, and smiled.

"Report, Archambault," the captain ordered, trying to look and sound official.

"A young boy found us on patrol, sir. He claimed that lives were in danger, including that of Monsieur

Klaus. We followed the boy and handled the situation."

The sergeant was sweating bullets.

"Sergeant?" asked Captain Archambault. He could sense that something wasn't being shared with him.

The sergeant smiled awkwardly.

The captain turned to his daughter, who gave him an all-too-familiar look. He knew then that something was bothering the sergeant, but his daughter didn't want him asking about it; she was handling it.

Deciding to move on, Gabriel asked, "Why was LeLoup shot?"

"I arrived on the scene just as he was preparing to shoot Monsieur Klaus," Egelina-Marie replied.

Gabriel's eyes opened wide. "Then what happened?"

The sergeant jumped in. "Sir, she shot him at a distance of at least three hundred yards. She shot him precisely in the shoulder, making him drop his pistol just before he could execute Monsieur Klaus. LeLoup fell to the ground immediately."

Gabriel was beside himself in disbelief. He'd had no idea how skilled she was with rifles. His wife had kept Egelina-Marie's secret to herself. "Three hundred yards... that's... that's nearly impossible."

"I know, sir," said the sergeant. "What's more amazing is that she arrived on the scene, and in one second realized what needed to be done—then took the shot. She shot from a standing position."

The captain looked at his daughter in amazement. "A snap-shot?"

Egelina-Marie smiled. "They've been calling me *Eg the Crack Shot*. Not bad for my first day, sir?"

Gabriel beamed with pride. "Not bad." Then he violated a few more pieces of his own advice and gave her a big hug. "You saved a very good man today, Egelina-Marie. A very good man."

"I know, Papa. I know," she said, hugging him back.

Egelina-Marie had left one thing out. When she and Nikolas had pulled Bakon off LeLoup, she had—for the briefest moment—exchanged a glance with Bakon and, ever since then... she couldn't get him out of her mind.

CHAPTER TEN
LICKING WOUNDS

The third floor of the treehouse was a six-foot square platform with a sturdy wooden railing. The view was breathtaking as the autumn sun touched the horizon and the adventurous day slowly retired.

The brilliant colors of the forest mirrored the mix of thoughts and emotions the yellow-hooded trio felt as they sat and thought about their day. They silently watched the leaves dance and the trees sway.

All of a sudden, Elly hiccuped loudly. She tried not to look embarrassed. Her hiccups were more like a bear roaring than a mouse sneezing.

Richy and Tee tried to ignore it and continue the thoughtful mood.

Once again, Elly erupted in a hiccup. This time she was a bit embarrassed. Richy and Tee broke their silence and giggled.

"It was terrifying," said Richy, looking out at the sunset.

"The hiccups or what happened today?" asked Tee, trying to resist the grin creeping across her face.

Elly, trying to head off the teasing, took control. She looked at Richy. "You saved the day, Richy."

Tee nodded in agreement.

Richy continued to look straight ahead. "Were you guys terrified too?"

"Yup," said Elly.

"Oh yeah!" answered Tee. "That hiccup was monstrous."

Elly reached over and punched Tee in the shoulder.

Richy smiled, nodded quietly, and then continued. "I was trying *so* hard to convince those guards to come. That older guard was just refusing and wanted to put me in jail if I wouldn't just go away. I was scared he was going to shoot the lady guard when she started to follow me, but I was more scared of you guys getting hurt."

"You know, when I got captured, I was really scared," said Elly. "I kept thinking that maybe I should have planned a little."

Tee turned and looked at her. "I'm glad you

didn't. There was no time. I was out of energy. They would have caught me if you hadn't shown up when you did. You guys saved my life, and my grandfather's. I don't know how to repay you... I'll never forget it."

They sat there in silence again, watching the sun dip a little further beneath the distant mountain range.

After a couple of minutes, Richy said, "You'd have done it for us, Lala."

"Yeah, only you'd have done it with more *style*," added Elly, grinning.

Richy sprang up and did an exaggerated imitation of Tee's signature gestures. "Oh, yeah, and about a half dozen *La-la's*! Fear not, for here I am! La-la! La-la! Fa-la-la-la-la!"

All three burst into hysterics. It felt good to laugh.

Tee stood up and leaned on the railing. "We have to head back before our parents wonder where we are."

As they started to walk down to the first floor, Tee said, "There's one thing I keep wondering about."

"What's that?" asked Richy.

"What was all of this about? I can't explain it, but I feel like there's something evil out there."

"In the forest?" said Richy, a bit confused.

Elly corrected him. "No—she means out in the world."

Tee nodded. "I feel like our fate is somehow tied to it. Does that sound crazy?"

"I know what you mean," said Elly. "I feel like today was some kind of test."

Richy took it in, and asked thoughtfully, "And we passed, right?"

"Time will tell," said Tee. "For all we know, this was only the first part."

Nikolas walked up to his daughter's log cabin. He was tired, but had cleaned himself up. He carried a bottle of wine, as he always did when he'd visit for dinner.

After wrapping everything up with the guardsmen and Captain Archambault, he was ready for a nice, normal evening with family.

Jennifer was in the front yard splitting a few logs with an old hand axe.

"Oh, hi Papa," she said. She wiped the sweat from her forehead and glanced around. "Where's Tee?"

Instinctively, he looked around, but then remembered. "Oh, she went off with her friends. She said she wouldn't be long."

Jennifer gathered some pieces of firewood from the ground, and then stopped. "You're a bit early," she said suspiciously. Her dad was notorious for being exactly on time. She studied him and her suspicion became concern. "I'll put some tea on. I can see you've had a busy day. Is everything okay?"

Nikolas gave a tired smile. "Yes. Yes, my dear. You don't need to worry about me."

Father and daughter entered the log cabin. Jennifer dropped the firewood in the pile beside the wood stove. She took a moment to warm her hands by the fire, and then filled the kettle and placed it on the blackened iron stovetop.

Nikolas pulled out a chair from the kitchen table and sat down. He loved their cozy, little home. It had two bedrooms and a main room. It was decorated with wonderful crafts. It radiated creativity and love.

Jennifer took after her mother. Nikolas and Isabella had moved a couple of times before settling nearby, and each time Isabella had managed to turn a house into a home within days.

"Hello? Papa?" Jennifer attempted to hand her dad a cup of tea for the second time.

"Oh, sorry," he said, smiling, accepting it carefully

with both hands.

"You know, Papa, you are a bad liar—at least to me," she said, sitting down.

He raised an eyebrow. "Am I?" He paused. "Well, Tee and I, we had some... excitement, today."

"Indeed. You're quite distracted." She took a first sip of her tea.

Nikolas looked at his own cup. "I fear, for some reason I cannot explain, that what has happened is not over."

"What happened, Papa?"

CHAPTER ELEVEN
IN SHEEP'S CLOTHING

A short, balding man in his fifties picked up his worn medical bag from the guard's inspection table. Nervous sweat pooled at the base of his hairline.

"Everything looks fine, doctor. You may enter," said the young guard, unlocking the thick wood and steel door leading to the jail cells. "This guy gets too much attention, if you ask me. After all these weeks, he's still getting people dropping by. Most guys only get one visitor, if any, before they're shipped off... or, you know, *executed*," said the guard with a slicing gesture.

The doctor forced a smile, making his round face look awkward. "Special circumstances," he replied as he hesitantly entered the small hallway.

"We moved everyone else to the jail across the street. You never know with a guy like this one. He's smart," said the guard as the doctor disappeared and the door closed behind him.

At the end of the hallway were three sparsely furnished jail cells. LeLoup was in the middle one, lying on its straw mattress and whistling.

Once the bolt of the heavy door was locked back into place, LeLoup turned to see who they had let into his cage—what fresh meat had they thrown him? It had been a couple of days since he'd had a visitor who wasn't a guard.

"Hello doc—oh, it's you. The *other* doctor," said LeLoup, pretending to be disappointed.

The doctor looked around, uneasy.

LeLoup continued, "If you're wondering if there is an echo in here, there is—from the stone walls. There's nothing to drink up the sound. It's why I like to whistle here—the echo. It does give the place an eerie feel, though. Of course, they wouldn't want it to feel like home, now would they? It would spoil the experience."

He sat up and stretched. "But you know all this already, don't you? It's not your first visit."

The doctor tried to hide behind his bag as he made his way to LeLoup's iron-barred cell door.

"How... how do you feel, Monsieur LeLoup?"

asked the doctor, adjusting his glasses.

In the weeks that had passed since LeLoup had been moved to the jail from the hospital, he had neither shaved nor brushed his hair. He looked like a wild man.

LeLoup's main doctor had stopped visiting a couple of days ago, saying everything was fine. When he'd last left the jail, he'd been complaining about how the Magistrate wanted LeLoup kept in such good health—a waste of the doctor's precious time given the prisoner was going to be executed anyway.

LeLoup had meant to ask him about this *other* doctor, but he had had so much fun terrorizing the poor man that he'd forgotten to do so.

With false graciousness, LeLoup said, "Doctor, I do so appreciate your visit. Without you, I'd have just these kind gentlemen to talk to," he said, gesturing to the empty cells. "I must say—they aren't as amusing as they once were."

The doctor frowned in confusion, looking to the other cells. "There's... no one there," he said quietly.

LeLoup stood up and exaggerated his own glance at each of the other cells. "Well, I think they *have* grown a bit thin—the food here is terrible. Even by local standards. Especially the cheese. Substandard."

Stretching once more, he stood up and found himself feeling a bit disoriented. Andre was vaguely aware that something inside himself had snapped that day outside of Klaus' house. He wasn't the man he'd once been. He felt freer and stronger—yet unbalanced, like a heavy club that could smash better but was harder to wield. Thoughts of revenge and restoring his reputation were increasingly dominating his thoughts; meanwhile, his long-held professional code of ethics was melting away.

LeLoup looked at the doctor. "I don't have many friends here," he said sadly. "In some ways, I've even abandoned myself. How about we declare that we are friends? What do you say? You could call me Andre and I will call you *Doctor*."

LeLoup tried to give the doctor his most charming smile, but he was distracted. When he'd said his own first name aloud, it had felt foreign, as if he had said someone else's name. He was only *LeLoup* now.

"Ah... okay," replied the doctor submissively, "but my name is—"

"You're name is Doctor! Don't demean yourself with a commoner's name, like *mine*. You are a special man—a smart man. You have devoted your life to an important profession. Allow me the honor of calling you Doctor?" LeLoup gestured dramatically, moving toward the bars. His intense, green eyes drilled into the doctor's own.

The doctor and LeLoup stood only inches apart, the iron bars separating them. LeLoup then leaned in further. His face pushed up against the bars.

"You are a doctor, right?" he asked, grinning disturbingly.

The doctor gulped hard and nodded. Sweat was running down his face and dripping off his chin.

If LeLoup had wanted, he could've reached through the bars and grabbed the frightened man, but he didn't.

He gave the doctor a sheepish look, and pulled himself back. "I've been too forward, haven't I? How rude of me. My mother always told me that all things come in good time. You can't rush a good thing like friendship. What do *you* think?"

The doctor lost his grip on his bag and it dropped to the floor with an echoing thump. He quickly wiped his sweaty palms on his pants.

"There's that echo," said LeLoup. He watched the doctor's every muscle as he bent to pick up his bag.

"So, how is my friend?" asked LeLoup, grinning. "That is why you are here, no? My friend, the horseman, visited you and asked you to pay me one more visit, didn't he? I can tell."

The doctor swallowed hard. He looked around in case somehow he'd missed seeing someone else in the room. "Y-y-yes," he stammered.

"Then we *are* friends. We should celebrate our friendship with a good meal. We could have some wine, some cheese, and whatever excuse they have for meat around here. What do you think?"

"Um, yes?" said the doctor, again confused.

In a disappointed voice LeLoup said, "But we have a problem. We cannot do this—not now. Do you know why?"

After a couple of awkward seconds, the doctor replied, unsure, "Because... you're in jail?" He had been stepping back and now found himself pressed up against the back wall.

"Oh—I thought it was because of my new look. Not fitting for a man of class, I suppose," said LeLoup, touching his face as he pretended to look in a mirror. He turned back to the doctor, grinned, and tapped his temple. "But you are right. A smart man! That's why you are the doctor and I am the prisoner. But now, as a friend, you will help me in a smart way, no?"

The doctor stared, expressionless, at LeLoup.

LeLoup dropped his smile. He opened his green eyes wide, almost as if they could swallow up the doctor. "*Right*, doctor?"

The doctor nodded mindlessly.

LeLoup relaxed his gaze. "Tell my horseman that I am being sent to the Magistrate tomorrow morning to be judged. He will know what to do." LeLoup stepped back, satisfied.

The doctor stood motionless, unable to decide what to do next.

"Leave!" commanded LeLoup. The doctor ran to the big door and banged on it repeatedly until the guard opened it.

"How did it go?" asked the guard.

The doctor slowly looked up from the floor to stare at the guard. His hollow eyes silenced the guard. The doctor then mechanically walked off to his scheduled meeting with Captain Archambault.

Tee was at home playing in the front yard when she spotted her grandfather coming down the road to the house. Planks of wood were sticking out of his cart, and she knew from experience it was likely filled with other materials as well. Nikolas regularly brought supplies over to build things with her and her father. The three of them loved it, and Jennifer loved watching them.

The closer Nikolas got, the more curious Tee became; it seemed he was pushing the cart—the kind that was supposed to be pulled by a horse. Something didn't make sense.

Before she knew it, she'd run up to him. "Grandpapa, what are you doing? You shouldn't be pushing a cart like that." She took a closer look. "Wait —how are you doing this? You aren't red in the face or sweating or anything."

He gently let go of the handles and the cart quickly stopped.

"Whoa," said Tee, amazed.

Nikolas smiled. "I was inspired, my Tee. The whole thing with LeLoup made me realize I cannot hide from who I am. Not from my involvement with the Tub, and not from my most important ideas. I must get them out into the world. If not, others will steal them and twist them to evil ends."

Tee nodded as she walked around the cart and then looked underneath. She marveled at the glowing blue lines that connected the strange, large box under the cart to the various wooden gears.

"Why does it glow blue?" asked Tee.

"Magic," said Nikolas with a twinkle in his eye.

"What?" said Tee, frowning at him. "You always said there's no such thing as magic."

Nikolas chuckled. "There isn't."

"What is it then?" asked Tee, excited.

"Hmm. Not just yet. Have a look first," said Nikolas, encouraging her curious nature.

Examining the handles, Tee asked, "How do these just stay in the air without falling or rising up? They're just floating there." She wasn't quite sure if she should touch them.

"Ah!" said Nikolas. "It's actually very simple. First, they are weighted and balanced independently from the cargo area of the cart. This cart is really two separate devices—connected for the purpose of movement."

Tee peered into the cart but couldn't see what he meant.

Nikolas continued, pointing, "Under this cargo area's floor is a hidden container filled with a heavy liquid. It keeps the cargo area perfectly level under normal conditions."

He could see Tee trying to figure this out in her head. "Get in. I'll show you!" he said, and offered to lift her up.

Tee hesitated before agreeing to go in the cargo area, among the tools and materials.

"Now, watch," said Nikolas as he thrust the handles into the air. He saw Tee's instinctive look of panic as she anticipated being tossed from the cart. Instead, nothing happened to her. She watched him arc the handles up and down, all the while the cargo area didn't move.

"Wow," said Tee as she climbed down. "Is the heavy liquid keeping it level because of—"

Nikolas made a fake cough and gave Tee his famous raised eyebrow. "My granddaughter, you have taught me that I should explain the dangers and the safety parts first—before explaining how the rest works, yes?" said Nikolas.

Tee smiled guiltily.

"So, do you think this is worthy of one of your *La-La's*?" asked Nikolas, continuing the walk to the house and pushing the cart with ease.

"Hmm, maybe," said Tee cheekily.

Nikolas took a moment to scratch his itchy, overgrown beard. He couldn't remember the last time he'd shaved, or washed properly. Isabella used to always make sure that no matter how much he was focused on inventing something, that he looked respectable, ate properly, and met life's other obligations. He missed her.

Tee took the handles from him and gave his cart a small shove. "This cart feels as light as my backpack."

Nikolas hid a yawn. "Yes. Do you realize that you are pushing fifty pounds of cargo plus the weight of the cart up an inclined plane! This one is *much* better than the one I first built."

"How long ago was that?" asked Tee.

"Years ago. I've been trying to figure out this puzzle of propulsion for a long, long time. I have *finally* solved it," replied Nikolas.

"Wow," said Tee again, pushing the cart a couple of yards.

When Nikolas yawned again, it was too big to hide from Tee.

She raised an eyebrow of disapproval. "Have you had any sleep, Grandpapa?"

Nikolas laughed. "You sound like your mother. You don't need to worry; I'm fine for us to make some sail-carts today."

Tee smiled approvingly. "One more thing," she said.

Nikolas squinted in mock suspicion. "Yes?"

"I won't say anything to mom about you not sleeping, *if* you let me push the cart the rest of the way home."

Nikolas folded his arms and pretended to dwell on the proposal for a bit. "That is acceptable."

When they arrived at the house, Tee's mother came out, wiping her hands on a towel. "What's this you've built, Papa?"

"I built *it*," he replied triumphantly.

"Built what?" asked Jennifer carefully, not wanting to assume she knew what he was talking about.

"He built a cart that doesn't need a horse!" yelled Tee. "I pushed it all the way from the dead tree to here... Me!"

Jennifer's jaw dropped. "Papa?"

Nikolas thought back to the first time he'd brought the idea up, a long time ago. He'd been enjoying a cup of tea and afternoon snacks with his wife, Isabella, and Jennifer, who was still a teenager. He had expected them to laugh, or be skeptical, but they hadn't. They'd taken the opportunity to tell him how much they believed in him, and if anyone was going to change the world, they knew it would be him.

"It took me longer than I originally thought, but yes, I got it working properly," said Nikolas. "It still needs a lot of improvement. I can make it last longer, be faster. I have many ideas I want to try."

Jennifer slowly moved around the cart and examined the contraption.

"Papa, these gears and the rest of the mechanism... It has evolved a lot," she said proudly. "The blue light! You always thought the energy would glow blue, but you couldn't ever get it to work."

Nikolas looked at his daughter, smiling. "So what ingredient was missing from my formula? Guess!" he asked her with a voice that reminded her of when she was a young girl. "You now know that it glows blue and that it works. My process hasn't changed from the one we discussed years ago. So what was missing?"

Jennifer crouched down and ran her hand along the glowing blue lines. "There's silver in this, isn't there?"

Nikolas nodded approvingly. "Go on. What was I missing in the battery solution?"

Closing her eyes, she built the machine in her head, as her father had trained her to do. She finally opened her eyes and looked at him with a silly grin. "Sugar," she said decisively.

"Such a smart girl," he said, beaming, a proud tear in his eye.

Unlike her siblings, Jennifer had been at his side while he worked on many of his inventions. Despite that, she never developed an interest in inventing machines herself. Her aptitude lay in other places— farming in particular. She managed to get more than twice the yield from her patch of land than anyone else in town.

"Sugar? Sugar does this?" asked Tee, confused.

Her mother and grandfather both laughed.

Jennifer answered, "No, Tee. What Papa has in there is a mix of different things. It reacts together and makes energy. What it had been missing to work properly was sugar. But I doubt it's anything like the sugar we use in the kitchen."

She stood up and looked her dad over. His face held triumph, and exhaustion. "You haven't slept in days, have you?" she asked, mothering him.

Tee giggled.

Nikolas tried to wave them off. "I have had *some* sleep. The body cannot function without *any* sleep, and the mind even less so. Now, is my body content with the amount of sleep I have given it? No. But I will sleep well tonight."

Jennifer shook her head. "Papa, you know what I mean."

Nikolas held her hands and looked into her eyes. "I had to get this done. Simon St. Malo thought I was working on the steam engine. That means he needs an energy source—a big one—to drive something. He probably means to transport huge numbers of cannons and soldiers.

"I did sleep at my workbench as I worked to solve the last piece of the puzzle. I *had* to make this. Something big is coming; I can feel it. I hope my invention will help our friends, not our enemies."

Jennifer listened thoughtfully. "Papa, let's talk about that another time. Right now, I'm really proud of you. Mama would have been proud too." She sniffed, resisting the sadness at the thought of her mother. With that, she gave her father a big hug.

After a minute, Tee realized something. "Hey," she said as the hug finished, "your library downstairs. You've already built something like this, haven't you? That's why it's always full of light."

A smile crossed Nikolas' face. "Not exactly, my darling granddaughter. But yes, that technology is a predecessor to this one. That room, I built when Grandmama was still alive. She helped me with it. It was my greatest invention at the time, and has always been a closely guarded secret. I only ever built one other, and like my house, it has an underground stream that makes it possible."

Jennifer took the towel from her shoulder, signaling she was ready to get back to work. "I'm sure you brought all this material so you two can keep Will out of trouble this afternoon?"

Nikolas smiled.

As Tee and Nikolas walked the cart to the backyard, Tee asked, "So how did you solve it, after all these years?"

Nikolas chuckled. "Always so many questions! I was sitting in my kitchen, having a cup of tea, reading my notes, and thinking—"

"Notes? The wood trim! So they are about this!" interrupted Tee, jumping up and down in triumph at having figured out the molding's purpose.

Nikolas messed her hair affectionately. "I learned that trick from my father, to hide things in plain sight. Like him, I like them to be beautiful, like the ideas they are hiding. Every time I had an idea I wanted to remember about this, I added it to the molding. When it was full, I took it down and made a new one that summarized the best ideas. I've done this many times over the years.

"When I put down my teacup, about to start taking down the molding, I knocked over the sugar jar. As the sunlight bounced off those wonderful crystals, the idea hit me!"

William was in the backyard and noticed them coming around the side of the house with the cart. "Hello, Nikolas," he said. "What can I help you two with?"

Nikolas' eyes twinkled. "Who wants to build some sail-carts?"

———

Captain Gabriel Archambault didn't love his job. As he'd risen through the ranks over the years, he had dreamt of what he'd finally be able to do when he became the top boss. The closer he got to the top, however, the more he came to understand how and why the captain's job was so tough.

It took an immense amount of energy to move the mountain that was the kingdom's bureaucracy. Gabriel suspected his predecessor had laughed all the way home after retiring, free of the *curse* of the job.

Two things he hated about his job were dealing with money issues, and complaints. People always wanted or needed things he couldn't afford to provide. The complaints were worse—if a kind soul said 'bless you' after someone sneezed, then a third person was at the ready to complain about it.

A knock came at his office door. Gabriel brightened instantly, standing up. "Ah! I am sorry— we're going to have to deal with this later." He looked at his staff—two men and a woman—all of whom were annoyed with him for kicking them out of his office at the smallest of excuses. They'd been hammering at him for two hours and he felt no guilt in showing them the door.

"Erin," he said, stopping one of his staff before she left, "now that the Magistrate has returned, I need him to answer those questions about the budget we sent over last month. Could you please go over and ask when will we have our answers?"

"No problem, Captain," she replied, and left.

With everyone having cleared out, Gabriel waved his next guest in and sat back down at his desk.

"So, *doctor*, how did it go?" asked Gabriel, rubbing his hands together.

The doctor seated himself. "You were right, Captain. LeLoup does have a horseman still out there."

Pausing for a moment, the doctor looked around

nervously. "We know one is dead and another we have locked up in jail, but there's still one out there. LeLoup thinks that horseman came to see me."

Gabriel smiled smugly. "He also thinks you're a doctor, lieutenant. Your plan was a good one. Can I assume he suspects nothing?"

The lieutenant paused for another moment, thinking very carefully about what he was willing to say. "Nothing, Captain. We're... way ahead of him."

Gabriel felt that his lieutenant was hiding something, and almost called him out on it, but decided not to. "Tell me what happened. I want hear what the man is thinking."

"Well," started the lieutenant, "I think he mentally cracked."

"We broke him? Already?" Gabriel appeared pleasantly surprised. "What makes you think that?"

"He hasn't shaven, his eyes look crazed, and the way he talks... it's different."

"He's probably so used to things going his way that one hiccup has torn his world apart. But this is just more of the same stuff you told me last time."

Gabriel had been disappointed then too. The lieutenant's first visit had been in the company of two guards, one of whom recognized the disguised lieutenant and had had a hard time playing along with the ruse. Before LeLoup could catch on, they'd left.

"What else?" asked Gabriel, leaning forward.

"Well," said the lieutenant, trying to come up with something, "he knows that he's going to see the Magistrate soon. He thinks someone will rescue him tomorrow afternoon."

"Really? Hmm. Anything else?" said Gabriel, disappointed.

"No," replied the lieutenant, looking at his feet.

———————

"This is awesome!" yelled Tee, racing down the mountain road toward her home. Her father and grandfather watched with pride as she expertly zigzagged around the bumps and stones in the road.

William loved seeing his little girl enjoying something they'd built together. "Pull the stick by your right knee. That's the brake!" he shouted.

As she pulled it, a wide piece of metal dug into the leafy dirt and brought her to a stop, right in front of them.

"This is better, yes?" asked Nikolas as he started to inspect the sail-cart.

Tee jumped out. "This is way better than the one

Elly and I put together. I like that the sail and mast can quickly go up and down. Having a brake is good, too."

Nikolas collapsed the telescoping mast and turned the sail-cart over. He checked the wheels and underside. "When you're on a hill, like this, you don't need the sail. Gravity will do all the work—unless for some reason you need to go very fast. With practice and a strong wind, you can even go up a reasonably inclined plane."

"Pardon?" said Tee.

"He means a steep hill," said her father.

"Oh," said Tee.

William switched to his dad-is-telling-you-something-important voice. "Now, Tee, remember that if you're going too fast and aren't careful with that brake, you could flip over."

"Dad, I had that figured out already," replied Tee cheekily.

"Hey," rebuked William.

Tee smiled apologetically. "Sorry—I got a bit carried away there."

William nodded. He loved that his daughter had spunk, but he felt responsible to make sure she understood where the border with being rude was.

He turned to his father-in-law. "So, how did this sail-cart do? As well as the others?"

Nikolas finished his inspection of Tee's sail-cart. "Hmm—I think I need to take this one back to my workshop. There's a... a wobble—in one of the wheels. I have a special tool there to help me fix it. I'll fix it and bring it back in a couple of days. You can take the others to your friends, Tee."

"A wobble?" repeated William, subtly unconvinced.

Tee was a little disappointed, but understood.

"Okay," said William. He knew Nikolas was up to something, but trusted him. "Now we've got to take a look at that old tree."

———

LeLoup chuckled to himself in his cell as he scratched his thick black beard. He joked with his imaginary cellmates. "Do you believe that last guard? All he had to do was give me my lunch, but no, what does he do? He gave me the rest of the information I needed and allowed me to recommend changes to the guard schedule."

"Oh, excuse me," LeLoup said, pretending to talk to the now-departed guard, "can you remind me who the hero of the day was again? That *was* an incredible shot. I wish to offer my congratulations—from one professional to another."

"Duh …" responded LeLoup in a silly voice for the guard, "that was the Captain's girl! She's new and her name is Egelina-Marie. She shot you really good."

LeLoup nodded. "Oh, yes, she did shoot me well. You know, guards like her are special. Can she come here, so I can congratulate her tomorrow at noon?"

In the silly guard voice, LeLoup answered himself, "Duh, no. She's going on a date with that Cochon brother, the one who pounded you. They'll probably go for a walk up the mountain while his brothers stay home. They live over at …"

LeLoup sat down on his straw mattress, laughing. "My friends, common people are *so* weak-minded. They are easily mesmerized, easily enchanted by words. These sheep… they forget that I am the wolf."

CHAPTER TWELVE

HOWLING FOR REVENGE

LeLoup woke to the sound of the heavy jail door opening. The morning sun through the barred windows partially lit the cellblock and started to warm up the crisp autumn air.

"Get up, LeLoup! It's off to the Magistrate for you. You'll be hanging by this afternoon."

LeLoup craned his neck to see who it was. "Oh! Captain Archambault, thank you for the wakeup call. I do believe I overslept."

The captain looked at the three guards who accompanied him and shook his head. "Can you believe him? Acting like we're taking him out for breakfast with the Queen." Two guards chuckled.

After an exaggeratedly long stretch, LeLoup stood up and brushed the straw off his dirty clothes. "Next time, please remind me to ask for a firmer bed. This one's too soft."

"Firmer?" said the captain. "There isn't anything firmer except the floor."

"Well then—I'll ask for some extra floor next time," said LeLoup mockingly.

His behavior bothered the captain. "You think you're so smart, don't you, LeLoup?"

"Think or know?" LeLoup snapped back. His green eyes were large and intimidating.

Gabriel grunted dismissively. "It takes more than big eyes to scare me." LeLoup was getting under his skin. "Open it up," the captain said to the guards. Two guards unsheathed their swords while the third unlocked the cell door.

Gabriel smiled at the prisoner. "Well, LeLoup, I'll have you know that we uncovered your plot with our pretend doctor. No one is coming to rescue you," said the captain smugly.

LeLoup wore an evil smile from ear to ear. "Really? A secret plot involving the doctor? And my third horseman? Whatever do you mean?" LeLoup stepped back and examined each of the guards closely.

"Out of my way!" commanded the captain to the guard who had unlocked the door. The captain stepped into the cell, quickly followed by the same guard. "The doctor was one of my men. We also made sure your *friend* who we have in the jail across the street has extra guards today. You are going to *hang*, LeLoup."

LeLoup shook his head mockingly and sneered, "Someday, maybe, but not today. You missed two things, dear Captain." His smile now looked even more sinister. "Who do you think convinced your good lieutenant to come out of retirement? Isn't it odd that he would *volunteer* such a plan? That he would be willing to come here to try and gather information?"

The captain was caught off guard. "Very funny," he said, uncertain. "Wait... I never said he was—"

"You never said he was a lieutenant, that he was retired, and that he came up with the brilliant idea? Oops, my mistake! This might be why I'm so bad at playing cards—I can't keep a good hand to myself. Would you like to go back to when you thought you had the upper hand?" asked LeLoup sarcastically.

"We're leaving!" yelled the captain to his men. "The Magistrate can come here for judgment!" He turned to leave, but the two guards, swords drawn, stopped his exit.

"You know, I actually had *five* horsemen. There's the dead one—tsk, a pity I had to kill him—then, the one you arrested, and the other one mysteriously close by. The other two? I ordered them to come here, some weeks ago, to join your guard corps. So, please, allow me to introduce my men," LeLoup said, gesturing to the guards holding the swords. "A small precaution, of course, in case I was ever arrested."

The captain stared at the men in disbelief. "No... it can't—" He looked to the guard who had unlocked the door. He was smiling coldly.

"And him? He's not a guard, either. I did tell you my third horseman was nearby. Probably closer than you were expecting." LeLoup licked his lips. "I do so love this game we play!"

———

Tee was the last one to come up the mountain pulleys. To her surprise, Richy and Elly were just standing there looking at the treehouse, some twenty yards away.

"What are you two looking at?" Tee asked.

Elly pointed toward the treehouse ramp. "At first I thought Richy was being silly, but he's right. Someone's definitely been here. No doubt about it."

Richy started walking toward the treehouse. "I'll show you what those magic elves have been up to. Look—a door, with some kind of lock," he said, gesturing dramatically.

Where the ramp to the treehouse's lower level had been, there was now a door. The door had a wooden puzzle embedded into it as a lock.

The three walked around the treehouse to see if there was any other way in. Circling back to the puzzle door, they confirmed that whomever had put it there had made sure they would need to solve it.

At first, the puzzle seemed impossible as some pieces could slide and others could turn, but gradually a pattern emerged. After ten minutes, they heard a clunking sound and were finally able to open the door. They didn't recognize the picture formed by the completed puzzle, or the meaning behind it, but they would, in time.

"Tee, I think your grandfather is the one who built this place and keeps giving us new stuff," said Richy as they started searching around.

Elly added, "I thought so too at first, but I don't think that anymore." She proceeded to open the cabinets and search their secret panels. "Hey! Come look at this."

Behind one secret panel were three new yellow cloaks. Another secret panel revealed six new shock-sticks and some other items.

"There's no way your grandfather could have

made all this stuff!" said Elly.

Tee and Richy each took one of the new cloaks, marveling at their quality.

"This is so light, but it seems dense at the same time," said Richy. "I mean—the fabric feels strong like it should be heavy, but it isn't." He held it up to the morning sunlight. "That's weird! The sun doesn't even come through it."

Tee examined the inside. "Check out all the pockets! I can put my slingshot here, and I guess the sticks go at the bottom edge of the cloak... maybe to give it more weight?"

"Or they could go in the special pockets right behind your back! Check them out," said Elly, pointing out the additional pockets she'd found.

Richy put his cloak on and asked Elly, "You really don't think Monsieur Klaus made all of this?"

"First," said Elly, "while it's been a couple of weeks since the LeLoup stuff, he's been preoccupied with something *big*. I've seen him in town twice, and he looked like a zombie. You know—the look he has when he won't stop until he's finished whatever he's working on. Tee, do you know what he's been up to?"

Tee smiled knowingly, but she wasn't going to answer. Her friends weren't surprised. They knew her grandfather often asked her to keep things secret until he was ready to share them. Yet, she liked how Elly deductively broke things down.

Elly continued. "Well—look at all of this stuff. The new sticks, for example. The design is a little bit different now. Do you think he really had the time to do that?" She played with the sticks in her hands, noticing that the balance was better and they were slightly thicker.

Tee thought about it. "Grandpapa likes to invent new things. These things aren't *new*. They're probably better than what we had, but they aren't new."

Richy made one last attempt to connect Nikolas to everything. "Maybe Monsieur Klaus has someone who works for him?"

Tee shook her head. She wasn't aware of anybody who had ever worked for her grandfather.

"Hmm," said Richy. "Well, right now, it's like we have little magic elves coming and making stuff for us. I'm okay with that."

Elly frowned. A troubling thought occurred to her. "This stuff means that someone knows who *we* are and that we come here."

Tee waved off Elly's concern. "I'm sure this is tied to my grandfather somehow, but it's not a mystery we're going to solve today. Until we see something worth worrying about, let's just assume it's someone who is trying to help us."

"Or *someones*," Richy added.

"That's not a word!" snapped Elly, rolling her eyes.

Bakon paced nervously. It was almost time to leave. He turned to his brothers and asked again, "Are you guys sure you'll be okay without me?"

Squeals looked at Bore. "Oh, I don't know," he said sarcastically. "Bore, do you think we might touch the stove and burn ourselves while he's out on a second date?"

Bore laughed. "Maybe we try to go outside and run into trees!" The two laughed for a bit.

Squeals turned to his older brother. "I think you're afraid she'll stop liking you because you're a low-life. She *is* too good for you."

Bakon hated the term *low-life*, and Squeals knew it. "We're poor, yes, but we make our own way. We always have," he retorted defensively.

He got up from their wobbly kitchen table and looked at the shack around them, now ten years old. They had been just teenagers when they'd built it, using skills learned from Monsieur Klaus.

During their time living with the Klaus family, they'd refused to live in the main house, except on the worst of days. At first, the brothers had insisted on staying in the large shed. Nikolas had fixed it up and insulated it. Isabella had come around to the idea since it forced Nikolas to deal with the mountain of stuff he'd been keeping in it.

The brothers had discussed the idea of their own home for months. When they'd finally decided to build it, they settled on a location about a mile away from the Klaus home. They'd still go over to have evening meals with the family every day, but afterward, they would head back to their own place. Unbeknownst to them, every night either Nikolas or Isabella would sneak over and check in on them before turning in for the night.

When they built their house, Nikolas had offered to help with more than just materials, but even Bore refused to allow him to do anything except watch, advise, and help steady the occasional beam. When the brothers were done, they immediately moved their few belongings in.

The house was very modest, but every leak and repair felt like a badge of honor. They were standing on their own and were proud of it.

Bakon bowed his head. "I just don't like the idea of leaving you guys." He felt like he was stealing something from his brothers in order to spend time with Egelina-Marie.

Bore shook his head in his exaggerated way and stood up quickly. He nearly hit the ceiling, as usual. "No," he said gently. "You scared of girl. Girl won't break up family. Maybe girl *become* family?"

Squeals and Bakon looked at Bore in surprise.

"Bang on, Bore! Eg and Bakon—sounds like a natural match to me!" teased Squeals.

With a quick glare from Bakon, Squeals quieted down. Bakon walked over to his youngest brother and looked up at him.

"Go," said Bore, warmly. His booming voice decided the matter. Bakon nodded.

As he walked out, he recalled how weird the first date with Egelina-Marie had felt at first. They'd met in the marketplace and just walked for an hour. Bakon had been so nervous he had rubbed his hands together until he had blisters. He hadn't noticed Egelina-Marie twirling her hair so much that she looked like she had braids.

To pass the time as he walked down the mountain

road, Bakon counted his coins and thought of what he would pick up at the market. This time he planned to have a picnic with Egelina-Marie. It would be simple, but it was all he could afford. Over the past two weeks, he'd done extra work for anyone who needed a hand, to earn the money he needed. His two brothers had insisted on helping but asked for none of the money.

Egelina-Marie was the captain's daughter, which weighed on Bakon. He couldn't imagine they would stay together long because, despite what he'd said to his brothers, deep down he believed that he really was just a low-life. *Someone like her shouldn't stay with someone like me*, he thought. He didn't want her to go —she inspired him and made him feel more *solid* inside.

"A man lost in thought," said LeLoup, startling Bakon. LeLoup stood in the middle of the road with three mounted horsemen, their pistols drawn. "You might not remember me. I've healed since our last encounter. But I remember you!"

Bakon was still a mile or two from the edge of town. He knew few used this mountain road at this time of day, so he was on his own. He stepped side to side, trying to prepare himself for trouble. "What do you want?" he asked.

LeLoup looked at his horsemen. "Hmm. Ruffians. They are always so rude." The men laughed. "I suppose we must be vulgar and get to the point immediately. You're lucky, Monsieur Cochon. I am not interested in lowering myself to your level and giving you the beating you deserve. I have a job to do."

LeLoup started to walk around Bakon, keeping a safe distance. "I will have my revenge on you, don't misunderstand me. On you, on the pretty Mademoiselle Archambault, on Captain Archambault, on Monsieur Klaus, and on those annoying Yellow Hoods who humiliated me. But… one thing at a time. Do *you* know what the next thing is?" he asked, stopping and glaring at Bakon with his piercing green eyes.

Bakon looked around quickly. "No. What?"

"It's obvious to the trained mind. But, again, you *are* a ruffian," LeLoup sneered.

He looked to his men and commanded, "Seize him!"

CHAPTER THIRTEEN

WHY, COME IN, MY DEAR

The main room of the house had turned into a staging area, holding the clothes and other items Tee's family were packing for their trip. Slowly, each item found its way into a large travel trunk or directly onto the horse-drawn cart.

"How long has it been since we last saw Aunt Gwen?" asked Tee.

Her dad walked in. "I think about a year and a half. I'm sure your cousin …" He paused, thinking.

"Elaine?" offered Tee.

"No, the other one. The little one," said William.

"Megan?"

"No, the younger one …" The name was on the tip of William's tongue.

"Honorine? Margo?"

Just then, Jennifer walked in, arms loaded with more clothes from the bedrooms.

"Your sister has a lot of kids," said William.

Jennifer laughed. "That sister of mine is a baby-making machine. Every time she sneezes, out comes another girl, and if she coughs, a boy! So far she's had six sneezes and two coughs."

"Dad's trying to remember the youngest one's name," said Tee, hastening the conversation.

Jennifer put her finger to her chin. "That would be... Catherine. Though you're probably thinking of Giselle."

"Wait—there's a Catherine now?" said William in disbelief.

"What's your point, Dad?" asked Tee, flopping backward onto a pile of clothes.

"I was just going to say she's probably grown a lot. You know—a lot taller and whatnot. But I got lost in all the names," he admitted.

Jennifer pulled a picnic basket out from behind the kitchen counter. "Well, Tee, here's something to distract you. Since we're going to be away for a month, I made some of Grandpapa's favorite foods. We'll be leaving at dawn, so would you mind heading over there now with this?"

Tee took hold of the heavy basket. "What's in here? Wood and rock soup?"

"That would still taste better than your Aunt's meat pie," said William, making his best yuck face.

"William!" snapped Jennifer, while trying to hide her smile of agreement. She believed strongly in respect of family and elders, especially in front of Tee.

"Sorry," he replied, chuckling.

"Hey, mom? Do you think one day we'll have a cart like the one Grandpapa made?" asked Tee.

"Oh, I have no doubt. I bet it'll go faster than a horse within a year," her mother replied.

"Alright. I'll be back for dinner." Tee donned her yellow cloak, checked her pockets, and headed out the door, basket in hand.

"Stay out of trouble," said her dad out of habit.

————————

Nikolas arrived at the guard administration building, a simple stone structure that housed Captain Archambault's office.

He opened the front door and walked through the rich, dark wood hallway to the reception desk.

The attendant's workday consisted of checking if people had an appointment, asking them to write their name down, verifying he could read it, and replacing the signature book when full. Unsurprisingly, he was asleep at his post.

Nikolas knocked hard on the desk, startling the man awake.

"Huh? Do you have a—oh, Monsieur Klaus. Can I help you?" said the man, rubbing his eyes and chubby face. He stood up to stretch his back.

"Yes," said Nikolas. "I'm here to see the Captain. I have an appointment."

The man seemed troubled. "Hmm, well... I'm sorry to inform you, Monsieur Klaus, but no one has seen the Captain since this morning."

"Oh," replied Nikolas, concerned. Gabriel had rarely missed an appointment with him. It was rarer still that Gabriel's staff didn't know his whereabouts.

"Thank you. I'll check at his home. Maybe, once again, he is sick, yes?" said Nikolas, turning to go.

"Actually, Monsieur Klaus, there is no need. We've had a guardsman drop by his home already. He's not there," said the man. "I'm sure he'll show up soon. If not, the Magistrate will have his head! Haha."

"The Magistrate? Wasn't LeLoup to be judged today?" asked Nikolas.

The man couldn't see the connection. "Yes, but according to one of the clerks who came by earlier,

they never brought LeLoup over to be judged. But"—
the man settled back into his chair while yawning
—"that's not my problem."

Nikolas knew one thing Gabriel would never do is
miss an appointment with the Magistrate.

"Which jail was LeLoup in?" asked Nikolas.

The man looked annoyed. "The north one. Why?"

Nikolas raced out of the building. He arrived out
of breath and immediately noticed that neither the
north nor south jail, on opposite sides of the street,
had a guard posted outside. He'd never seen that
before. He banged on the door of the north jail and it
swung open. He stepped in cautiously.

"Hello!" he yelled. "Is there anyone here?" He
listened carefully. He heard something down the
corridor, toward the cells. "Gabriel, is that you?" he
called loudly.

"MMMMMM!" came a muffled reply.

"Gabriel!" yelled Nikolas, rushing toward the
cells.

He found Gabriel bound and gagged in one of the
cells, and a guardsman face down and tied up in the
next cell over. Nikolas raced over to free his friend.

"That wretch!" boomed Gabriel, rubbing his
wrists. "We've got to go after him!"

Nikolas hastily went to make sure the other man was alive, and then untied him as well. He then returned to his friend. "Why hasn't anyone noticed you here?"

Gabriel's mood worsened. "Do you want the truth —that my people are lazy and deserters? Or, that for the past three years the Magistrate has refused to give anyone a raise or pay for proper equipment? There are so many reasons why they just sit on their behinds unless the proverbial bear comes right up to bite it."

Nikolas laughed. "Better I not ask?"

"Mmm," grumbled Gabriel. He took the hand Nikolas offered, and stood up. "What time is it?" he asked.

"Late afternoon. Why?" replied Nikolas.

Gabriel dusted himself off. "LeLoup got out this morning. He's planning revenge on everyone involved. Especially some 'yellow hood' character."

———

Tee usually took one of two routes for getting to her grandfather's house. The shortest way was through the forest and took about twenty minutes on foot. The other route went past Elly's house and was much longer.

"Hey guys!" yelled Tee as she came down the

road.

Elly and Richy were racing their new sail-carts. Tee was surprised how fast they were going. Despite it being slightly up hill, they were going at least as fast as she could run, if not faster.

"Wow, that looks fun!" said Tee, putting her basket down.

Elly yanked her sail and pulled the brake, quickly coming to a stop.

Richy, showing off, picked up even more speed.

"What are you doing, Richy?" asked Elly.

"Watch this!" he yelled. Richy pulled down the sail and telescoping mast, tucked himself into the body of the sail-cart, turned the steering wheel hard, and pulled his brake. The sail-cart flipped sideways into the air!

Elly and Tee both watched in horror and amazement. At just the right moment, Richy popped up from inside the sail-cart and landed it expertly. As soon as the sail-cart's wheels touched the ground, he raised the mast and got it quickly moving again. A couple of seconds later, he came to a decisive stop.

Richy's heart was pounding. "Was… awesome? How was …?" he said, trying to catch his breath.

"Breathe," said Elly as she and Tee ran up to him.

Richy took a deep breath. "Wasn't that awesome? It's my best one yet!" He got out of the sail-cart and found his legs were wobbly. "I think I'll sit down for a minute."

"That was awesome," said Tee, grinning.

Elly leaned over him. "Is that how you got those scratches and bruises on your head and arms? You told me you fell out of a tree," she said disapprovingly.

Tee cocked her head, siding with her best friend on this one. "Richy, she's got her arms crossed and her brow down. You'd better fess up. Come clean," warned Tee, gesturing for Richy to give up the goods.

He sported a winning, toothy smile and asked Elly, "So—was that impressive?"

She thought about it for a moment, and then nodded. "Yeah, it was," she admitted, cracking a smile. "Just make sure you don't hurt that pretty little head of yours, okay? The rocks in there need a nice place to live."

Tee and Elly laughed, and Richy smiled.

"So, Tee, are you guys leaving tomorrow?" asked Richy, standing up and stretching his legs.

"Yes indeed. We're off to see my aunt. But first I'm going to Grandpapa's house to drop off some goodies," replied Tee.

"Which aunt—the one with a million kids? The rich one? Or the—" asked Richy.

"The one with a million kids," replied Tee. "I know you have no cousins or anything, but if ever you wanted some, just let me know—I'll give you tons. I'll give you some too, Elly."

"No thanks!" said Elly, waving Tee off. "I have enough cousins. Not too few, not too many."

Richy chuckled. "I still remember when your aunt visited a couple of years ago. You could hear her kids all the way down the mountain!"

Tee sighed. "There are even *more* of them now. My mom said she has eight kids."

"Eight?" said Elly and Richy, stunned.

"Wow," Elly continued, "that's a lot of baby smells... and screaming."

Tee knew that, unlike herself, Elly wasn't a fan of babies. Tee loved playing a big sister role. "Anyway, I'll be gone for a month."

"A month?" asked Elly, never liking it when they were apart.

Tee paused in thought. "I think that's what my dad said. About four days there, four days back, and two weeks with my aunt's family. Add in maybe some bad weather or maybe a side trip to the capital city for some chocolates, and that's a month."

Elly almost leapt on Tee. "Westria? Are you seriously going for chocolates in the holy place of tasty treats?"

"My mom said we *might*—she means if I'm really good and everything goes according to plan," said Tee.

Richy snorted. "Forget it, then. Nothing ever goes according to plan."

Tee looked up to judge where the sun was and how much afternoon she had left. "I'd better get going, guys. I've got to drop this basket off at Grandpapa's so I can get back home before dark."

"Hey," said Elly, "why don't we sail along beside you?"

"Actually," said Richy, "Elly, if you'd let her piggy-back on the back of your sail-cart, I think I can handle the goodies."

"Okay," said Tee, "but no flips please. I smelled an apple pie in there."

———————

"Do you know what the best part is?" asked LeLoup, crouched down beside the bound and gagged Bakon. He'd been unceremoniously dumped on the floor near Nikolas' kitchen doorway, and was now glaring at LeLoup.

LeLoup smiled menacingly, his eyes wild. "Shall I continue, or did you want to make a point? No? Nothing to add? Good. I'll continue.

"Simon St. Malo will get what he wants, boosting my reputation further and making me a *very* rich man. I'll still need to eliminate any rumor I was beaten and jailed in this nowhere-land, but that comes with the territory. Anyone with sense will believe it was all part of my plot to defeat a member of the Tub.

"The old me wouldn't accept allowing things to get as messy as they are going to get. I'm free from that now—thanks to you, and Mademoiselle Archambault, and Monsieur Klaus, and that infernal, yellow-hooded granddaughter of his. I do so look forward to your deaths."

The front door opened, and two of LeLoup's horsemen walked in. LeLoup stood to look. His men had Egelina-Marie, tied up and fighting wildly.

"Ah, here we go," said LeLoup. "One girlfriend. Slightly scrambled. Drop her beside him. You, guard these two. You, I want you on patrol. I've already got your colleague guarding the back."

Deciding he had some time on his hands, LeLoup

went to the kitchen. "Monsieur Klaus," he said to himself, "you have such a fine selection of tea. I think I will enjoy some more. I have to say—this cozy kitchen is growing on me."

LeLoup made his tea and then sat down. He looked around the kitchen. He looked at the walls. Gradually, he looked up at the ceiling, all the while ignoring the muffled yells and the sounds of futile flailing around by Bakon and Egelina-Marie. Then, it hit him—the crown molding, that wooden trim at the top of the kitchen walls that he'd admired last time, had been removed and replaced with simple, smooth wood.

LeLoup put down his teacup. He stood up on a chair and rubbed his hand where the crown molding used to be. "So there it was, telling a story. My little story, now where did you go? Hmm?"

———————⌒———————

Richy, Elly, and Tee rapidly approached Nikolas' house in their sail-carts.

"Tee, I can't believe you haven't been able to drive your sail-cart yet," said Richy.

"Yeah, what's the deal with that? It's been a while. Is he building you a *new* one?" asked Elly.

Tee got off the back of Elly's sail-cart and

shrugged. "I don't know. I would love to have it but I know my grandfather has a good reason... I just don't know what it is yet.

"By the way, that was a great wind we had behind us! It was certainly faster than walking with that big basket." She accepted the picnic basket back from Richy.

"When you're going against the wind, you can use the sail just like on a ship and tack side to side into the wind. It's really cool," said Richy.

"Huh," said Elly, impressed. "I hadn't thought of that. How do you know about sailing?"

Richy smiled. "My dad took me sailing a couple of times this summer. Since this had a sail, I figured it would work the same, and it did."

"Hey, look—there's *my* sail-cart," said Tee, pointing. It was sitting just outside the open doors of the large shed.

After the Cochon brothers had moved to their own house, Nikolas had reclaimed the shed, once again filling it with a million things from rakes, to old cabinets, to things unknown.

"It doesn't look any different," said Richy. "I would have thought he'd at least paint it yellow or something."

Tee shrugged. "I'll have to ask him. I can't imagine he's done *nothing* to it. Anyway, thanks for the ride, guys."

Elly raised her sail and her cart immediately started to move. "Richy, I'll race you home!"

Tee waved goodbye to her friends then walked up the path. She climbed the steps to the front door. A bad feeling washed over her, and she looked around. Deciding she was being silly, she knocked on the door. A minute passed.

"Odd," she said to herself. She went down the steps and reached around underneath them. "Hmm… No big rock, so that means he's not home." She looked at the open shed door, confused.

A decade before, Nikolas had developed a simple system to let his family know whether he was home or not. If he was home, he'd leave a large rock under the first step. Only once had he ever forgotten. Tee knew the door to the shed was always closed when he wasn't home—without exception.

She went to the front door and knocked again. Another minute passed. She checked for the rock again, this time on her hands and knees. The bad feeling got stronger.

She stood up, cleaned herself off, and yelled,

"Grandpapa? Are you in there?" She waited, fidgeting nervously.

Just as she was turning to leave, a reply came. "Come in!" yelled a distant, muffled voice.

With her hand on the doorknob, Tee hesitated. It didn't sound right. "Grandpapa? Is that you?"

"Come in my dear!" yelled the faint voice again.

The hair on the back of her neck stood up. She backed down the steps and then along the path a couple of yards. She donned her hood, pulled out her shock-sticks, and gave one of the handles a few quick turns.

"Are you coming in?" called the muffled voice, closer now.

She glanced around, waiting nervously, and started winding up her second shock-stick.

The door creaked open.

"I said *come in*," growled the voice.

———————

"I win!" yelled Elly, pulling her brake and popping out of her sail-cart. "I beat you! I beat you!" she taunted Richy while jumping up and down in the middle of the road. It had been an exciting race home.

"Fine, I was beaten," said Richy. Noticing something behind Elly, he pointed and said, "Hey—"

Elly glared at him and interrupted, "Don't rob me of my victory!"

"But—" said Richy, still pointing, now waving his finger.

"No buts!" said Elly.

"But *us!*" said Captain Archambault as he, Nikolas, and a contingent of ten armed guardsmen ran up to them.

The kids sprang to attention and saluted the captain.

"Don't do that," he replied, waving them to stop. "Save that for the Magistrate or someone whose ego needs it." He hated that the kids were taught to do this. He understood the tradition, and had done it himself as a child, but it bothered him now that he was the one being saluted all the time.

"You know, my friend," said Nikolas, trying to catch his breath, "you are in remarkably good shape for—"

Gabriel started to laugh. "For a fat man? Ha! I'm running on anger. I'm sure I'll drop dead when this is over."

Towering over Richy and Elly, the captain said, "We need to find your friend Tee. Have you seen her?" His voice was clear and commanding.

"We just left her... at *his* house," said Richy looking at Nikolas, confused. "If you're here, then ..."

"LeLoup!" said Richy and Elly in unison.

"Do your parents have any horses?" the captain asked Elly. "LeLoup and his men made our horses sick. We ran here. We believe that Tee and others are in danger."

Elly replied, "My parents have two horses, but Richy and I can get to Monsieur Klaus' fast on our sail-carts. It doesn't take long, especially with the wind today."

"What's a—" started Gabriel. He then turned to Nikolas. "One of your inventions?"

Nikolas nodded. He was looking somewhat recovered.

Richy ran off. "I'll be back in a second!" he said to Elly. He came back a moment later with their yellow cloaks, which they had left by her front door.

Captain Archambault turned to two of his men. "Inform this young lady's parents we'll need to borrow their horses, and then get to Klaus' house as fast as possible."

He turned to Elly and Richy. "You kids go *now*. Go as fast as you can. Your friend's life is in danger. If you see any of LeLoup's men, don't do anything—just wait for us. But if you see her, quietly get her to come to you.

"The rest of you, let's go! Nikolas, what's the fastest way by foot?"

CHAPTER FOURTEEN
OF HOOD AND WOLF

"I said come in," repeated LeLoup, with sinister playfulness. He emerged from the house, into daylight, and walked down the front steps. Like his men, he wore dark red, leather armor. He sported both a sword and a gleaming pistol in his belt.

"Things never go according to plan, now do they?" said LeLoup, disappointed. "Here I was, waiting for you to come in, and you so rudely decided to stay outside. Mind you... it *is* such a nice afternoon." He looked at the leaves and trees for a moment. "The forest seems almost in conflict between yellow and red, don't you think? You, obviously, representing yellow— which is fine with me, as I do so love red," he said, grinning menacingly.

Getting no reaction out of the yellow hood-covered figure, he continued, "Last time, when my men were working so hard to capture you, you Yellow Hoods pulled a deceitful switch on me. That was rude —clever and well executed, but rude.

"That sort of cleverness could lead to something. With the right guidance and tutelage you could become a force to be reckoned with. I've seen it before. The old me would have maybe made you an offer, but now? I'm not interested in letting you go any further."

Tee took a couple steps back. She wasn't sure what to do, or what to expect. Her heart was racing and she was sweating.

LeLoup kept trying to peek under the hood, but to no avail. "Now, the question on the top of my mind is —with whom am I dealing? Do I actually have the granddaughter of the great Monsieur Klaus in front of me—or do I have one of her two friends? Oh, are you wondering how I know there are three of you? Those jail guards are talkative. Dangerously so—for you."

All of a sudden, LeLoup leapt forward and tried to grab the hood, but Tee matched him with a quick leap backward. Her hood remained in place, continuing to obscure her scared face.

"Well done," he said with genuine appreciation. "You have good reflexes. But, I'm running out of time. Time, time, time." He sighed and drew his pistol, pointing it at Tee.

"This," he said, showing off his pistol, "is a mature cousin of the ones still popular in these parts. It has better balance, better accuracy, and far less recoil. Next time I'm home, my multi-shot pistol should be ready. Oh, if only I had it now... I'd love to show it to you. It is a marvel of modern technology—like the new rifles, but small and elegant." LeLoup flexed his fingers for a moment to make sure he had a good grip.

Tee went from nervous to panicky. LeLoup noticed her shock-sticks shaking.

"Not so brave now, are you? I'll have you know this pistol is loaded and ready. A shot from this distance will go clean through you and leave a hole the size of... well—best I not panic you too much." LeLoup savored the moment.

That afternoon, he'd spent a half-hour in the glowing library downstairs and an additional hour going through the rest of the house, book by book, note by note. He had found nothing of value. The only drawings he'd found that he could make sense of were for a ridiculous, four-wheeled, small cart-like contraption that had a mast and sail.

It boiled LeLoup's blood to think that Klaus had

outsmarted him by hiding out in the open, but it enraged him even more to think that he'd wasted his time pursuing someone whom he wanted to believe was really just a clever fraud. He would be humiliated if he returned with nothing.

LeLoup took a step forward. "I'll make this simple, child. Show me where Monsieur Klaus has built the steam engine, or find me that missing crown molding from the kitchen—I know it has *something* to do with all of this. It has to. Why else would it be gone? I won't ask again!" His jaw visibly clenched.

Just as Tee thought she might pass out from fear, a wave of confidence and calmness washed over her, and a response bubbled up from the back of her mind. Making her voice lower than usual, she replied, "Moldy crowns? Well, I can offer you an old princess dress, but I don't think it's your size!"

LeLoup was completely taken aback. "Are *you* mocking *me*?" With his free hand, he unsheathed his sword. "Mocking *me*—the *great* LeLoup?! Do you have any idea who you are dealing with?"

"I thought you were the *okay* LeLoup, or was it the *adequate* LeLoup? It doesn't matter… now that you've tangled with the Yellow Hoods, your name is mud!" said Tee with biting confidence. She felt like the words were saying themselves, and she was just listening to them.

LeLoup started twitching. The machine that was his mind had lost another bolt. He tried to compose himself, but his arms started to shake. He tightened his grip on his sword and tried to steady his pistol arm. *"Enough!* Give me what I want or I *will* shoot you. Then I'll shoot the Captain's daughter," he said, gesturing to the house. "Then Cochon. And then I'll shoot"—he paused, trying to muster up the calmness to lie confidently—"your grandfather."

At first, when LeLoup mentioned hostages, Tee felt her courage start to dissolve, but then she realized —something didn't sound right. She remembered the rock under the steps, and the open shed.

"Well, since you don't *have* my grandfather, are you planning on shooting any other imaginary figures? Fairies, perhaps?" Tee paused to measure the effect of what she'd said.

She knew that he might very well have some hostages, but resisted the urge to trade her surrender for their freedom. She didn't believe he'd really let them go. She didn't even know if her grandfather had what LeLoup was looking for in the first place. So she pressed on. "You're a fraud, LeLoup. Your reputation, your sense of superiority—it's all a sham." She crouched down, like a spring being coiled.

LeLoup was having trouble thinking straight. He was incensed and struggling with his emotions. How dare an impudent child mock him? How could his great career come down to a standoff with a *child?*

His desire to win by superior intellect was losing ground to his need to prevail by any means necessary. In his rage, he could no longer remember why he'd avoided bloodshed on his earlier missions. *It must have been weakness*, he thought to himself.

One of LeLoup's horsemen galloped by, yelling, "We have company!"

LeLoup—his mind on fire, and face red with rage —glared at the Yellow Hood

From behind the house, a gunshot rang out. LeLoup instinctively turned to look.

Tee seized the moment. Pressing the hidden button on one of her shock-sticks, she sprang forward. With one stick she knocked the sword out of LeLoup's hand. The other she jabbed into his chest. A few sparks flew, but he seemed unaffected. She immediately regretted not having practiced more with them.

He laughed, and sprang back. "I *knew* this armor

would work!" He fired his pistol.

"Tee!" screamed the other two Yellow Hoods as they careened around the corner in their sail-carts.

LeLoup smiled from ear to ear, feeling in control again. "So I *do* have the granddaughter." Looking down at the crumpled yellow heap, he said, "If you aren't dead yet, give me what I want or you will be!" He picked up his sword.

Elly brought her sail-cart to a quick stop and sprang out, while Richy picked up more speed in his.

LeLoup looked up, confused, as Richy's sail-cart rapidly approached.

"Aaah!!" screamed Richy. He yanked down the sail and telescoping mast, swerved, and pulled hard on the brake. Still moving very fast, his sail cart flipped into the air.

"Richy!" screamed Elly, frozen in place.

The sail-cart soared higher than ever before and crashed into LeLoup's chest, sending him flying backward.

Richy landed his cart expertly on all four wheels and brought it to a sudden stop. He hopped out, wanting to help Tee, but stumbled to the ground, dizzy and trying to catch his breath.

Elly, meanwhile, helped Tee to her feet.

"I'm okay," said Tee. "The cloak absorbed the bullet! It scared me, but mostly it just knocked me off balance."

"That's amazing," said Elly, looking at the cloak.

"You're not hurt!" said Richy and Tee, to each other.

"Look out!" screamed Elly as LeLoup rose and staggered over to retrieve his fallen pistol.

Tee sprang forward and unleashed a battle cry from deep within, "Aaaaaaaaaah!" With both hands around her remaining charged shock-stick, she ran at LeLoup and forcefully struck him right in the chest. More sparks flew and this time LeLoup flailed and dropped to the ground.

Elly let out a big sigh and collapsed gently to the ground. "I don't know how much more of this I can take," she said, laughing nervously.

Tee picked up LeLoup's pistol and tossed it toward the shed, followed by his sword.

Richy chuckled and looked at Tee. "By the way, we came to tell you… LeLoup escaped from jail."

"Really? Thanks for the heads up," replied Tee sarcastically, but with a smile. She picked up her other shock-stick, which had fallen when she'd been shot. "Why didn't this one work properly?"

Elly took it, cranked it furiously until she couldn't anymore, armed it with a quick press of the hidden button, and then struck the ground with it. It released a shower of sparks, and left a black scorch mark. "Maybe you didn't wind it up enough?"

"Tee?" yelled a voice from behind the house.

"Here!" Tee replied, her nerves calming at the sound of her grandfather's voice.

The sound of a shot from the doorway shattered the moment. The Yellow Hoods turned to see a horseman pointing his rifle at them.

"Don't move!" he commanded. "I've got a second shot in this, so don't move a muscle. Now—"

Just then, the horseman who had raced by earlier came galloping back. Upon seeing the three Yellow Hoods, he charged his horse directly at them.

"Run!" screamed Tee.

"No—*sail!*" corrected Richy. He grabbed his sail-cart, giving it a running push before leaping in.

Unmoving, Elly locked steely eyes with the rapidly approaching horseman, pulled one of her fully charged shock-sticks from her cloak, armed it, and threw it at him.

His eyes widened as he recognized the object just before it made contact. A moment later, he was on the ground, flailing about—for a second time, thanks to Elly.

Elly and Tee grabbed their sail-carts and followed Richy toward the main road.

In all the confusion, the horseman at the doorway fumbled his rifle and accidentally fired into the trees. Out of shots, he started running toward his fallen colleague.

"Forget him! Help me!" barked LeLoup. Quickly, the horseman got LeLoup to his feet and hastily led him away.

"Tee?" yelled Nikolas as he arrived on the scene, only to see a downed horseman, and the three Yellow Hoods in their sail-carts heading down the road. He bent over to catch his breath, sweat beading down his face.

Captain Archambault arrived a minute later. He put his hand on Nikolas' shoulder to reassure him, and was about to say everything was going to be fine, when LeLoup and his last remaining horseman came galloping through in pursuit of the Yellow Hoods.

CHAPTER FIFTEEN

To the Ends of the Earth

Elly, Richy, and Tee raced past two dismounted and wounded guardsmen who must have tangled with a horseman earlier. The astonished guards didn't understand what the kids were yelling as they raced by. A moment later, LeLoup and his last horseman bolted by in pursuit. The guards looked at each other, not sure what to do.

As the Yellow Hoods zoomed down the road, Elly hollered, "Richy, I've got to say, that thing you did with launching your sail-cart at LeLoup—"

"That was crazy," interrupted Tee.

"Insane, that was just insane," finished Elly.

Richy smiled. It hadn't been the plan—it was just instinct, as if his sail-cart was an extension of himself. He would have done anything to protect his friends.

He suddenly had a bad feeling. Wanting to get a

good look at the road behind them, he gave a quick jerk of the steering wheel and a pull of the brake for a second, before letting it go. His sail-cart spun around so he was now facing backward. Richy felt one of the wheels start wobbling.

"You can do *that?*" exclaimed Elly.

"LeLoup!" yelled Richy, deftly spinning his sail-cart back around.

Tee and Elly glanced over their shoulders. Their stomachs tightened with fear as they saw LeLoup and his horseman galloping after them.

"They're gaining on us!" yelled Elly.

"Richy, any idea how we can charge our sticks and not crash?" asked Elly. "I've never sailed this fast."

He looked at the simple controls of the sail-cart. "Um, um… okay, I've got it! Bring your sail down, and use your knees on the steering wheel—like this!" Richy started to furiously wind up his shock-sticks. Elly copied him.

Recognizing a distinctive gnarled tree and large rock, Tee realized they were near where she and Elly had tested out their first homemade sail-cart, weeks ago.

Glancing over her shoulder, Tee confirmed LeLoup and his horseman were only a dozen yards behind. She shot a quick look at her friends. Their weapons were ready, and sails back up. Taking a deep breath, Tee made her decision.

She pulled her hood back, revealing herself, and turned to lock eyes with LeLoup. His face became red with rage as he recognized her. Tee turned her sail-cart off the road and into the forest. LeLoup immediately followed.

"Where's she going?" screamed Elly. "What's she doing?"

The horseman still pursuing Richy and Elly fired his pistol— but missed both of them.

Richy glanced back and threw his first shock-stick at the horseman. While his throw missed, it caused the horseman to drop his pistol.

The horseman was almost on top of them now. He pulled out his sword. Reaching down, he swung the blade in a wide arc, cutting Richy's sail in half. As Richy tried to maneuver, two of his wheels fell off and the sail-cart spun out.

Elly looked at her remaining shock-stick. Recognizing she was almost in front of her own house, and knowing the next section of road like the back of her hand, she took a chance and stood up in the sail-cart. She turned backward to face the grinning horseman as he prepared another swipe—and then expertly threw her shock-stick at him.

"Bull's-eye!" yelled Richy as he saw the horseman flail and fall off his horse, rolling into the bushes.

Elly sat back down, yanked down the sail, and pulled hard on the brake, bringing her cart to an abrupt stop.

After taking a moment to catch her breath, Elly looked up to see her parents standing outside— staring in awe at what they had just witnessed.

They looked at the riderless horse trotting by, then Richy, who was cheering as he ran toward Elly, and then back to their daughter. They weren't sure what to make of everything.

Elly climbed out of the cart and smiled at her parents. "Sorry—I can't talk about it. Official *Yellow Hoods* business."

"Huh," said her parents, dumbfounded.

⸻

Tee needed to maintain strict focus in order to control her sail-cart as she rocketed down the mountainside. The last time, she had taken advantage of every opportunity to slow down. This time, she tried to go as fast as she could—LeLoup was trying to run her down. She could hear him screaming incoherently behind her.

Meanwhile, back at Tee's home, William and Jennifer had just finished loading the second trunk onto the cart.

"I think that's everything," said William. "I can't believe that even with all of the stuff out here, the house *still* looks pretty full."

"Do you hear something?" asked Jennifer, glancing about.

William listened and looked around carefully. "Sounds like it's coming from over there," he said, pointing.

"That sound... I can't figure out what it is," said Jennifer.

What had started as a single, rumbling noise quickly separated into a concert of distinct sounds: tree branches snapping, underbrush being crushed, wood knocking on stone, a horse whinnying, and a familiar high-pitched voice calling out.

"Get the crossbow!" yelled Jennifer. *"Now!"*

"Huh? Why?" said William, though he reacted immediately and started to search.

"It's Tee!" said Jennifer.

"Are you sure?" replied William, confused.

"*Yes!* Something's wrong!"

Both of them searched furiously for the crossbow and the bolt with the rope attached.

"Why can't we ever remember where we put that thing?" yelled William, frustrated.

Over the noise came Tee's desperate voice, "Mom! Dad! Help!"

Jennifer was almost paralyzed by the screams of her baby girl. "Will, I've got the bolt with the rope! Quick—she'll be here any second!" Jennifer started to track where Tee might be coming from.

"Got it!" yelled William, sprinting from the other side of the house, crossbow in hand.

Jennifer handed the bolt to her husband. "Someone's chasing her!"

William yanked the string back hard with one hand, cocking the crossbow.

"She's coming too fast, Will!" said Jennifer, panicking. "Slow down, Tee!" she screamed.

After placing the bolt in the crossbow's barrel, William aimed for where Jennifer pointed, awaiting his exact target. The seconds seemed to stretch out forever until, in the blink of an eye, Tee shot out of the forest and across the clearing, with LeLoup only a few yards behind.

William was beside himself. "The cliff—I—I didn't have time," he stammered quietly.

Before any emotion could settle in, Jennifer yanked William's arm and yelled, "Come on!" They darted after Tee.

Seconds later, they heard a horse's prolonged neigh, a loud crash, and then silence.

———————————

As Tee re-entered the forest across the clearing, she realized her parents couldn't save her this time. She was closing in on the cliff.

When the familiar tree came into view, Tee remembered how she, her grandfather, and dad had reinforced it, tying it back with the cables her grandfather had crafted, and packing down the roots with more soil. Her grandfather had also secured a mysterious iron ring to the tree, at about his shoulder height. He'd measured where it was to go a half dozen times, and after installing it, had tried his best to pull it out, but it held firm. He hadn't explained why he'd attached the ring. All he had said was, "I put it here just in case."

Tee pulled the sail-cart's brake with both hands, but sensed it wouldn't be enough at this distance. There must be some other way, she thought, her eyes desperately searching for an answer. Then, she noticed the other lever, similar to the brake on the right, but on the left. It hadn't been there before. Grandpapa!

With nothing to lose, Tee pulled the second lever with all her strength. Suddenly, five mini-crossbow bolts shot out of the front of the sail-cart, trailed by thin black cables. As her grandfather must have expected, one connected with the tree's iron ring, and —like magic—locked itself securely in place just as Tee and her cart went sailing off the cliff.

The horse, upon seeing the cliff edge, neighed with panic. It violently turned and started back up the mountain, throwing LeLoup into the air.

He grinned at the thought that Tee would share his fate—but then the slack in the cable ran out and both Tee and her sail-cart flew through the air in a semi-circle, and back onto the cliff's edge.

"No!!!!!!" screamed LeLoup.

A moment later, Tee's parents arrived to find their daughter face down in the dirt and leaves. Her sail-cart lay a few yards away, smashed and tangled in cables. To their relief, Tee rolled over and looked at them with her beautiful large brown eyes.

After repeatedly checking herself for injuries and hugging her parents, Tee said, "I guess LeLoup won't have to worry about people knowing he was defeated by the Yellow Hoods."

Her parents chuckled with nervous relief.

"You forgot something," said Jennifer.

"What's that?" asked Tee.

"Your triumphant *La-la*," answered her mom, sweetly.

Tee thought about it for a moment. For years, Tee had added her special exclamation to things she'd done—but none of them had been as serious as this.

Sitting on her dad's knee, and looking at the trees and their enchanting, colored leaves, she said, "Mom, I think I might have outgrown it."

Her parents hugged her tightly.

CHAPTER SIXTEEN

TALE OF THE YELLOW HOODS

From the moment that Jennifer had proposed to everyone to bring their families, and some food to share, the hours had flown by. The evening was a victory celebration. Almost everyone made it.

After eating, Jennifer gathered the group around the wood stove and retold the tale of the recent events. In her captivating tale, she deftly wove together everyone's perspective. Though they all knew the outcome, she held her audience in suspense the entire time. This telling would cement the story in everyone's minds as the first tale of the Yellow Hoods.

William had coordinated the food and beverages, and kept the fire going while Jennifer regaled everyone with the tale. He was fond of watching his wife tell a great story.

As a side tale, she explained to Tee the long-standing relationship between the Cochon brothers and the family. Tee apologized, again, to Bakon for the stone incident.

Nikolas sat quietly during all of it, cuddling his granddaughter. He thought to himself how these gatherings helped make the house a home.

He'd watched Bakon and Egelina-Marie with fatherly pride. Each was unsure how to act with the other in front of family, friends, and neighbors. Gabriel and his wife seemed to be oblivious to the whole thing.

Bore and Squeals reminded Nikolas of when they were little and would sit by the fire with his other children, while Jennifer would capture their imagination with wild bedtime stories. Now they sat there, bigger, but still boys, soaking in everything and laughing at the best parts. Isabella would have loved to have seen it.

Nikolas felt Tee's head gently slump against his arm, and gave her a nudge. "Okay, my dear, we must get you to bed now."

Tee nodded slowly, her eyes barely open. Nikolas stood her up and guided her to her bedroom.

She sat on the bed and let her grandfather pull off her socks. She lay down and he pulled her covers up and tucked her in. He gave her a kiss and was about to leave when she said in a sleepy voice, "Grandpapa …"

"Yes, my dear?" he replied softly.

"No one answered my question," she said, turning over and propping herself up with a pillow. Light from the main room silhouetted her grandfather, preventing her from seeing his face.

"What question was that?" asked Nikolas softly.

Tee yawned and closed her eyes. "Did—" she said sleepily, "did anyone find LeLoup's body?"

Nikolas leaned on the doorframe in thought for a moment. He started to answer, only to be interrupted by the sounds of Tee's deep breathing.

"Tee?" he asked gently.

There was no reply.

He smiled and whispered, "You've had a busy enough day."

Before returning to the main room, Nikolas pulled a small red box out of his pocket. He'd waited long enough. Carefully, he opened it.

He removed an encoded note and what looked like a special bath plug. The plug was made of steel and had divots around the edge.

Nikolas had wanted to provide a way for the Tub

to communicate securely. Almost as a joke, he had designed both the "bath plug" key and a machine which could use it to encode and decode letters. To his surprise, it had become an immediate hit with the members of the society and had been in use, with little modification, for the past ten years.

He examined the divots on the plug's perimeter, mentally building up the list of which letter or letter combination decoded to which other letter. With the decoding key in memory, he then read the note.

He gently rubbed his forehead and then tugged lightly at his newly trimmed beard as he digested the message and its implications. After a moment, he put the plug and letter back in his pocket, planning to destroy them before the evening was done.

Nikolas looked again to his granddaughter, sleeping peacefully. "I fear the world will need you and the Yellow Hoods sooner than I'd hoped," he said with dismay. With that, he quietly closed the door.

CHAPTER SEVENTEEN
RISE OF THE HOUND

It had been a long, painful road, but the dark figure was determined and tenacious. If word got out he was still alive, he was sure he'd be hunted down. Fear helped drive him, but more than anything, he wanted to stop being a *nobody*.

The echoes made by his heavy, tattered boots on the marble floor were almost deafening. The long, poorly lit corridor provided little distraction from the sounds of his rhythmic pace—a pace he'd kept up for weeks. No matter how exhausted or how much pain he'd felt, he'd forced himself forward.

The glint of the gold trim around the huge double doors at the end of the corridor finally came into view. His stomach tightened. He knew he'd be putting his life in the hands of a man known to be untrustworthy —known to use people up, and then dispose of them.

Still, he pressed on.

His knock on the great doors was followed by silence, his heartbeat his only company.

As he waited, he finally noticed the paintings and statues decorating the corridor. When he looked at them, he felt nothing inside. He'd stripped away so much of who he'd been to get there; he couldn't remember if he liked art of any kind. He wondered how many other things he'd walked past without taking notice, how many other things he didn't care about anymore.

Finally, the enormous door creaked open. A bald, sickly looking old man in fine brown and green attire stuck his head out. He slowly examined the figure before him, from head to toe and back. The old man wrinkled his nose at the sight and smell of the visitor, but then showed him in.

The visitor had a grizzly, dirty, red-brown beard and hair that hadn't seen a brush in weeks. His face had caked-on dust and sweat. His clothes were torn and dirty.

Entering the room, the nameless man was taken aback by its grandeur. It had the look and size of a royal library—though he'd never actually seen one. He could imagine two or three hundred people milling about in the space.

The outer walls were covered with gold-embossed bookshelves that reached all the way up to the thirty-foot ceiling. There were stairs on wheels, and ladders here and there—all to provide access to the highest shelves. Inside the room, eight-foot-high bookcases were arranged throughout, almost making smaller rooms within the grand room.

There were three stunning, dark wooden worktables covered with drawings, as well as several antique couches and chairs. The floor was a polished, icy-white marble with flecks of blue and green. He had never seen anything like it.

The immense chandelier, which hung in the center of the room, cast light everywhere. With the reflective marble, and freestanding oil lamps positioned perfectly throughout, all shadows were eliminated. Side tables had books stacked in perfect piles. Everything was methodically arranged.

A man wearing scholarly robes seemed to appear out of nowhere, almost as if he had slid out from behind a bookcase.

"Incredible, isn't it? This is my sanctuary," he said. He was a clean-shaven man with salt-and-pepper hair, and about five-foot-eight-inches tall and likely in his late forties. His fine robes were a luxurious purple and had detailed gold and silver embroidery.

The finely dressed man quickly assessed his guest. He let an uncomfortable moment pass before introducing himself. "I am Simon St. Malo, inventor and advisor to the regent of this kingdom. Come, please—let us sit, and let us be *civilized*."

Simon St. Malo was a master of word choice and tone. The words he chose were inviting, yet his tone made it clear he was looking down on the nameless man. His guest bowed his head slightly and then followed. Simon secretly smiled. He liked that his guest was obedient. What he didn't like was that he looked and smelled like a dirty, mangy dog.

St. Malo was making the nameless man's skin crawl. He wondered what devil's bargain he was about to make, but it was too late to turn back now.

Simon gestured for his guest to sit in a chair—a chair which he was certain cost more money than the guest had seen in the past year. Simon made a mental note to have the chair burned later, figuring there was no good way to rid such fine upholstery of the reek of *wet dog*.

"Cleeves, some tea please," Simon commanded. He turned to his guest. "Do you drink tea? If you don't, you should. It is said that tea is good for one's health. Besides, Cleeves isn't useful for much, but I do appreciate how well he can boil water and pour it onto dry leaves. Asking him to bring it gives him a sense of purpose in life."

Simon, himself at ease, purposefully let his guest wait in uncomfortable silence.

Eventually, the old man arrived with the teacart. He poured fresh, hot tea slowly over a strainer and into each of two teacups he'd set out on the cart. He carefully handed each man a cup and saucer, motioned to the assortment of biscuits and other items, and left as quietly as he had come.

Simon used silver tongs from the teacart to inspect a piece of crystallized raw sugar. Deciding it met his criteria, he lowered it carefully into his teacup. He watched it start to dissolve before stirring it gently with a small ornate spoon.

Seeing that his guest did not wish anything in his tea, Simon clapped for his servant. Cleeves returned and took the teacart.

After enjoying his first sip, Simon broke the silence. "I've been told you dragged yourself down a mountainside to the town of Mineau. From there, you walked for days until you stole a horse from a farmer

—leaving the man stranded with a plow in the middle of his own field.

"That first horse, you rode until it couldn't move anymore. They say you then walked until your feet bled. And when a man stopped to help, you beat him until he gave you his horse. Is this all true?" Simon asked, leaning forward a bit, trying to hide his eagerness. He studied the man as he awaited his response.

The nameless guest looked down at his tattered stolen boots. Hidden inside were his badly cut and blistered feet. He then looked up at Simon, his face confirming everything and more, without saying a thing.

"You took his boots, too?" said Simon, smiling. "You're committed, driven. You *are* a loyal dog," said Simon, leaning back. "Blind devotion to the idea of coming here. I like that."

Simon looked around for a moment, in thought. He had a look of surprise as an idea hit him. "Cleeves!" he called out. "Make a note regarding the new pistol design. I should make the handle wider by a half inch. I'll remember why. Have you noted it?"

"Yes sir, I'm noting it," replied the old man from somewhere in the room.

Simon's mind was always working on several things at once, and Cleeves was often the man to catch the thoughts Simon tossed out for his later reference.

"Well—he's done two things right in one day. I should make a note of *that*," said Simon snidely to his guest. "When genius strikes, it is our responsibility to capture it, no?"

The man, his tea untouched, looked at Simon with dead eyes and nodded. With a man like St. Malo, not responding might be unsafe, even when the question seemed rhetorical.

After taking a couple more sips of tea, Simon placed his teacup and saucer down. "I can understand coming all this way if you were Andre LeLoup himself, as it is literally his head on the line. But you... you were *just* a horseman. Why go through this trouble? Where is LeLoup, anyway?" he asked.

The man decided that before he'd answer, he would take his first sip of tea. Despite not having ever enjoyed tea before, this tasted somehow like... success. Though that didn't make much sense, he decided he wanted more of it and what it represented.

"LeLoup's dead. Went off a cliff," he said in a low, hoarse voice. He had barely spoken in weeks. He took another sip of tea, and then looked for a place to set it down. He noticed that while St. Malo had a side table, he hadn't been provided with one. This couldn't be accidental. He could see another side table, oddly placed off in the corner. He realized St. Malo subtly treated his guests this way to make them uncomfortable.

"Hmm," said Simon. "Dead? Unfortunate. I didn't take Nikolas Klaus for a killer. I guess we all evolve. I have underestimated him in the past."

The nameless man gently shook his head. "It wasn't Klaus. It was"—the man paused, swallowing his nervousness—"the Yellow Hoods."

"What's a *yellow hood*?" asked Simon, irritated. He didn't like it when topics came up that he didn't know everything about.

The guest looked at St. Malo, and then at the ground. He wasn't sure how to say they were *just three kids*. He was certain that St. Malo would be furious and perhaps have him killed.

"The Yellow Hoods are a group—disciples of Klaus. They protect that area now," he said after having thought about it. Simon could detect there was more to the story, but for the moment, he was satisfied.

"Moving on—" said Simon, "I see no tube or

crumpled plans under your… *excuse* for a shirt. Am I missing something?"

"No."

"Well, then," continued Simon, "I take it that you were too stupid to run and hide? Are you like a dumb but loyal dog who has returned to his master, only to be shot?"

Simon then leaned forward, pretending to examine the man's neck. "I wonder how many hacks it'll take for that head of yours to come off? The axe is dull, I'm afraid—the result of budget cuts. We just can't seem to find the money to sharpen it. It takes longer, being dull—but it still works."

The man leaned forward, causing Simon to recoil slightly. "I came because I want to *matter*," he said forcefully.

"What could you possibly *have* that would make me think you matter?" asked Simon. Everything hinged on what the nameless man would do next.

"I brought you something," said his guest finally, looking back at the ground.

Simon didn't believe him. "Really? What could you have brought that could possibly change my mind?" He hated having his time wasted. It was bad enough when people he needed did so, but this disgusting peasant? "Dog, what do you have?" he asked angrily.

The wounding words bounced off the man. He knew St. Malo's reputation, and that he had reached the end of his patience. He pulled out a short metallic rod with a small handle at one end and offered it to his host.

"What's that?" said Simon, gesturing to it with disgust. He refused to take it.

The man started to crank the handle. "I don't know, but it was powerful enough when thrown at me by a Yellow Hood to shock me right off my horse. I couldn't get up for ten minutes. My body still hurts when I think about it. The handle cranks, but I'm not sure what else to do to make it work. I think it came from Klaus."

Simon gracefully snatched the rod out of the man's hands, and stood up to examine it. "Well of *course* it's something interesting. But, hmm ..." Simon turned the rod over in his hands, examining the handle and other features. "Nikolas has had something to do with it—of that I'm sure—but this isn't his alone.

"This is an *excellent* prize. With it, you have shown me not only what he is up to, but potentially with whom he is working. My dog, it seems you have brought home a very good stick. It wasn't what I asked for, but it was what I wanted."

"So ...?" said the man, wanting to know his fate. His exhaustion was showing.

Simon put the short rod down on the side table and looked at the man with an offended expression. "Do you really think I'd get rid of a tenacious, loyal dog that has an eye for good *sticks*?" He revealed a sliver of genuine appreciation for his guest.

Simon looked at the rod again. "I'll give you a third of what I was going to pay Andre LeLoup—plenty more than you're used to. You might even be able to afford one of these chairs— used, of course." Simon lifted his head, as if talking to the ceiling. "Cleeves—pay the man," he commanded.

"Yes sir. One third of the amount noted for Andre LeLoup," said a bored voice from somewhere in the room.

"Thank you," the man said quietly.

"Now, then—burn those dreadful clothes once you are out of here. Disgusting, really. Not befitting any man," said Simon, frowning.

He looked again at his new toy, sitting on the side table. This was an unexpected turn of events. He turned back to his guest with a piercing look. "I have need of a man like you. Provided I get your undying loyalty and devotion, I can give you what you want. What *do* you want?"

"I want to matter," the man replied.

Simon waved away the answer as nonsense. "Oh, you'll matter. But what is it that you *want*?"

"I want those Yellow Hoods on my wall," said the man, releasing a tiny fraction of his anger.

"A motivated man. Excellent. What's your name, dog?" asked Simon.

"Call me... The Hound."

Enjoy this excerpt from Book 2 - Breadcrumb

Trail.

CRUMBLED PLANS

The Hound stood back up and rubbed his head as a dark April rainstorm beat down. He'd landed hard on the slick stone rampart, yet had managed not to slip off or black out. Rain poured off his brown and beige leather long-coat.

For a moment, he looked concerned. He glanced at the control boxes on his forearms and the connections to his oversized, metallic, gear-covered gloves. He hoped rain wasn't getting in. Satisfied, he turned up the dial on each forearm's control box. Electricity started to jump and crackle between his fingers. He then turned his attention back to the Yellow Hood at his feet.

The yellow-hooded Tee dangled below the half-built rampart, desperately clutching her slingshot. When she'd slipped, its leather strap had caught between two of the moss-covered stones. She could feel her hands slipping as the rain wormed its way between her fingers to moisten the slingshot's wooden handle. She looked down and swallowed hard.

The plan sounded bad from the start, but they had trusted the leader of the Tub. It was bad enough to be asked to go deep into the Red Forest, to an open area with an unfinished, crumbling castle tower and half-built rampart wall—never mind the leader's unwillingness to tell them why they were going there in the first place. Once the opposing secret society's coach had arrived and the representative for the Fare had stepped out, the plan fell apart.

Tee shot a glance around to look for her fellow Yellow Hoods. Elly, with her gray metal shock-sticks in hand, was dodging and blocking a red-hooded swordsman's thin blade. Richy couldn't be seen.

"Lights out, kid," said the Hound. His gloves crackled and electricity danced from finger to finger.

Tee took a deep breath. She could only think of one option, and it was risky. She freed one hand to delve into her yellow cloak's hidden pockets. Pulling out a shock-stick, she pressed its activation button while staring into the Hound's eyes. He hesitated.

"You've *enjoyed* this before, haven't you? Care to do so again?" Tee said menacingly. She wasn't sure if she was willing to risk the fall to the cobblestone below.

Suddenly, Tee's pinky finger slipped off the end of her slingshot. She could feel the other fingers slipping, too. Then, a glint of steel from an arrow aimed at her from less than twenty feet away caught her eye.

The red-hooded archer smiled and said, "Goodbye, little yellow birdy!"

THANK YOU
FOR READING THIS BOOK

Reviews are powerful things. In addition to sharing your thoughts and feelings about the book, your review lets the rest of the world know that there are people reading the book.

Many people don't realize that without enough reviews, indie authors are excluded from marketing and newsletter opportunities that could otherwise help them get the word out.

So, if you have an opportunity, I would greatly appreciate it!

Don't know how to write a review? Check out AdamDreece.com/WriteAReview. Where should you post it? Your favorite online retailer's site and GoodReads.com would be a great start!

Thank you,
Adam

ABOUT THE AUTHOR

Starting The Yellow Hoods was one of the best decisions I've ever made. In taking a leap of faith and kicking off my indie author career, I ended 25 years of doing nothing with my writing, and transformed that *one day I'll be an author* thinking into *now what?*

The first world I remember creating and sharing with others was as a little jean-jacket wearing five year old at a park. I described for my friends, Tatiana and Simon, the imaginary realm we suddenly found ourselves in. We ran around using our fingers to shoot lasers and jumped on our Big Wheels to fly off through space.

I live in Calgary, Alberta, Canada with my awesome wife, amazing kids, and lots and lots of sticky notes and notebooks.

I blog about writing, life and more at **AdamDreece.com**.
Join me on Twitter **@adamdreece**, on
Facebook at **AdamDreeceAuthor** or
send me an email **Adam.Dreece@ADZOPublishing.com**

BOOKS IN THE SERIES

Along Came a Wolf
ISBN: 978-0-9881013-0-2

Breadcrumb Trail
ISBN: 978-0-9881013-3-3

All the King's-Men
ISBN: 978-0-9881013-6-4

Beauties of the Beast
ISBN: 978-0-9948184-0-9

Watch for Book 5, coming Fall 2016

COMING SOON

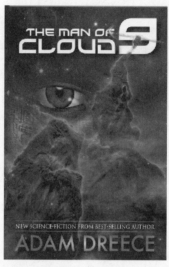

The Man of Cloud 9
ISBN: 978-0-9948184-3-0

A science fiction tale of a high-tech
startup genius, his conscience, and the
corporate beast he created.
Suggested for readers 12-99

Autumn 2016

ENVIRONMENTAL BENEFITS STATEMENT

ADZO Publishing saved the following resources by printing the pages of this book on chlorine free paper made with 100% post-consumer waste.

TREES	WATER	ENERGY	SOLID WASTE	GREENHOUSE GASES
12	5,677	5	380	1,046
FULLY GROWN	GALLONS	MILLION BTUs	POUNDS	POUNDS

Environmental impact estimates were made using the Environmental Paper Network Paper Calculator 3.2. For more information visit www.papercalculator.org.